SUBJECT
TO
CHANGE

SUBJECT TO CHANGE

LOIS GOULD

Farrar, Straus & Giroux

NEW YORK

Library of Congress Cataloging-in-Publication Data
Gould, Lois.
Subject to change.
I. Title.
PS3557.087S77   1988   813′.54   88–352

C 1175.

SUBJECT
TO
CHANGE

gift has come for you, said Henry. It is from your sister.

My sister? Let me guess. A nightingale. One of those that flit about in a gilt cage, pretending to sing.

Henry smiled. Not even your sister would dare that more than once. As I recall, you smashed the last one and sent back the feathers, one at a time.

Well, Catherine mused. Lace, then. Yards of hideous lace. For a gown I will never wear.

Will you pout, Catherine, or will you receive your gift? I have other business this morning.

Very well. Leave it. Go to your business. Go to your mistress. Go to—(Morgantina has entered the room, curtsying)—dear God, the queen exclaimed. What is it?

A frisk of nature, my love. Like you.

By now the queen was too busy inspecting her gift to take offense.

She raised its skirts. Henry! It's extraordinary. A tiny monster. A gargoyle.

Yes. Upon occasion, your sister will send the perfect thing.

3

Does it speak—do you speak? Catherine poked the creature here and there.

Certainly, madam, said Morgantina. I am quite speechful.

Henry, what shall I ask it?

The king shrugged his shoulders and stepped back, edging toward the doorway.

Have you wit? whispered Catherine, giving the creature a tentative pinch. Do you play at sport?

I am sport, said Morgantina.

Are you impudent? Shall I test her? Henry, don't leave me with—does she bite?

The king sighed. I cannot stay. I am sure she'll do no harm. But test her with care, Catherine. She is said to be a witch. Your sister would surely send us a witch.

Catherine went on prodding and pinching. The dwarf, accustomed to these attentions, endured them without changing her expression.

What were your parents? Catherine chattered. Have you brothers? How do you sleep? Do you dance? Are you chaste?

I sleep cross-legged, Morgantina replied. With my toes in my ears. So saying, she dropped abruptly to the floor and assumed this pose, which transformed her into an intricate ball of colors.

Look, Henry! cried the queen. How does she do that?

No one can tell how, my lady, said the dwarf, and she commenced to roll. Faster and faster she tumbled across the checkered marble floor, bumping into corners, propelling herself backward as though flung by an unseen hand. A rolling dwarf may always find a place to sleep, she explained. In case anyone comes, they will find me like this, with my head between my feet, resting on them

4

as on a pillow. I tuck my great toes inside my ears, like this, to make the world a better place. You know, I am the only one who can do this trick with my body; it may frighten the king, but the queen will boast of it one day, laughing to the ladies of the court. Ssh, now!

The dwarf's eyes slowly closed; her voice became light and soft, as in song. I see a shadow, she murmured. It is there, across the bar of yellow light beneath my door. It is the queen; she has come to whisper about me. She must tell her guests of my cleverness and my monstrosity. She must say she has never owned a thing so clever and so monstrous as I. They will not necessarily envy her for this, but for other things: her perfume, her red jewels, this dreadful great castle. She must hang a great work of art over my bed; it will be a portrait of me by an unknown artist. Behind me in the painting, a mound of quicklime smolders as rain falls upon it. When quicklime is watered down, it burns strangely and shows its fire, though there is no flame. Heaven weeps. The queen never weeps, you know. And the dwarf never shows her fire.

nce there was an unhappy young queen who loved her dwarf better than monkeys; better than rose-colored brocade or Greek myths spun in sugar; better than the music of her own praises sung by poets and fools. Each day the queen and her dwarf would play a game of who can tell, in which the queen must try to guess the ending, and must always be surprised. The dwarf, for her part, knew that the ending was subject to change, just as she was. Each day the corridors of the palace rang with the dwarf's silver laughter and the queen's red cries of rage, though many swore it was the other way around.

One morning the queen decided to play a trick on the dwarf, by pretending to be tired of the game. Let us try something else, she said, in a tone of disarming sweetness. Morgantina, for that was the dwarf's name, cunningly agreed. Forfeits? Word portraits? Riddle me this?

The queen, whose name was Catherine, frowned her darkest frown. Let us play life and death, she said. You are smaller and uglier, so you must go first.

Morgantina leapt nimbly off the game table, kicking her tiny feet high into the perfumed air. The queen laughed as one miniature slipper flew off in a circle, landing toe-up on the lowest-hanging arm of a candelabrum with twenty crystal branches. There it swung, twinkling in the lights like a magical white fruit. The other slipper soared and circled in the opposite direction, ending on the splendid long nose of a white marble goddess of wisdom. There it drooped, shivering like a delicate silver snivel.

You lose! said the queen, brandishing her gilt-laden sewing scissors, and snipped off both the tip of the dwarf's odd little nose and the top of her dear little arm, just at the shoulder. Morgantina murmured respectful apologies, and rearranged her expression.

Now it was Catherine's turn. She rose from her crimson throne, rustling her taffetas, sweeping her priceless tea things to the floor. Shards of rare porcelain roses suddenly bloomed in the marble squares; rivers of heavy cream, golden honey, scarlet jam, flowed into the silken tapestry carpets, creating new races of brown spotted unicorns, doves with crimson wings, and thick amber huntsmen whose arrows dripped red while still in their bows.

You lose again, sighed the queen, sounding a trifle bored. She chopped off three handfuls of Morgantina's amber hair, one breast, and half her thick red smile.

Alas, whispered Morgantina, two cannot play at this game.

How clever you were not to think of that before! said Catherine, folding her hands.

With that, Morgantina sprang to her bare feet, seized the gilded shears, and held them pointedly over Catherine's heart. With your Majesty's pardon, the dwarf said, in a most beguiling voice. Snip, snap! She drove the point home. Catherine cried her reddest rage; the dwarf laughed her laugh of purest silver, each knowing how the other loved a surprise ending.

The next day all was well. The dwarf's severed parts

had grown back, thanks to the salve of Seven Thieves' vinegar which she always tucked in her silk purse in case of emergencies. The queen's heart, though it had softened dangerously in the night, was hard as new before the first cock's crow. She felt it carefully all around, before rising and clapping her hands. The dwarf appeared. What shall we do now? Catherine demanded crossly. She made her black brows meet in the middle, for emphasis.

Why, who can tell? replied the dwarf, concealing her merriment. The queen dimpled in spite of her displeasure. Play it yourself, she said. I shall sit in judgment or stand on ceremony, depending.

The dwarf curtsied very low, using the time to think. Then she drew herself up to her full height, which was exactly as high as a queen's very low curtsy, if a queen ever had occasion to curtsy.

Are you willing to sit for your portrait? asked Morgantina.

Certainly not, said Catherine. That would put me nearly as low as you.

The dwarf wrinkled her odd little repaired nose, noticing that it still smelled new. Thinking made her look much uglier, which caused the queen to laugh.

Will you stand for your portrait, then? said sly Morgantina.

No, I won't stand for it! shrieked the queen. By then she was laughing so hard that the dwarf managed to draw a green moon for the face (the queen had a sallow complexion, owing to her Mediterranean birth; two small dark eyes, much too close together; and a turned-down mouth with one snaggle tooth). Paint box, palette and brushes, along with the sketch, vanished into Morgantina's silk purse before the queen could compose herself.

We are not amused, said the dwarf quickly; she was only fooling. The queen boxed her eyes just in case, and slit her tiny tongue crosswise. She had forgotten (or perhaps not) that the dwarf's salve of Seven Thieves' vinegar was poisonous if taken internally. The royal tailor had to be summoned; twelve tiny stitches taken in Morgantina's foolish tongue; a golden thread plucked from the queen's own second-best silken cloak. Even so, Morgantina was unable to utter another jest all evening; her cold supper, beaten to a froth by thrushes' wings, had to be sipped through a glass straw as fine as a royal hair. The queen was furious.

As luck would have it, a great necromancer arrived that very night at the palace gates, begging a crust of fresh bread for a cycle of stale madrigals. This fellow, Cornelius Agrippa by name, also dabbled in rhyme, theology, astronomy; in heresy, alchemy and love. He had lately served a philandering prince; before that he had read Plato, failing to win tenure at eight great universities. He had tried numismatics and satire; a duke commissioned him to build a fine theater and write a series of new comedies for it. He plagiarized a series of old comedies instead, but only three authors were alive to complain, and two of them had been plagiarists as well. Now Cornelius had fallen on hard times, forced to make his way across Europe, from kingdom to dukedom, juggling golden balls and metrical eulogies; a sonnet here, a parlor trick there.

He had learned to lose nobly at cards, allowing unscrupulous merchants to cheat him royally. He could sing to the lute and advise an ambitious courtesan on the art of collecting poets. He could flatter an ugly duchess for an entire afternoon, while she sulked before her looking-glass. In better days he would strut the streets of wonderful cities, in scented gloves, a rose behind his ear, a pocket edition of stolen rhymes swinging coyly from his belt. He was blessed with sorrowful eyes and a lost dreamer's mouth, so that every lady loved him a little, especially while he read her stars and painted her portrait in Latin verse.

Cornelius had traveled on foot a hundred weary miles from his last dreary palace to this one, having heard that the young queen had a sad face and an open hand. A juggler who once flattered Catherine in the street boasted that he had won a fine supper and a damask coat. And in the taverns where mediocre rhymesters gathered to embroider their tales, Cornelius learned that this queen had a dwarf by whom she set great store, and that, in fact, one who amused the lady Morgantina might beg any favor of the mistress.

As he trudged from town to dusty town, Cornelius learned all he could of the queen and the dwarf, so that he might prepare for their meeting. He must invent extravagant compliments and set them in brilliant rhymes; he must find a way to read the future in a dwarf's palm. He must polish his wit to shine like new-minted coins, or the smile of a sorcerer. All this he would offer the sad queen and her creature, in exchange for supper and the lease of a cottage for as long as they wished him to stay.

At one village, he happened upon a baker who made gingerbread dwarfs in the likeness of her Majesty's favorite. All who had seen Morgantina herself swore that these confections bore an uncanny likeness; the hump in particular was a triumph. And there were many ready to testify that if one nibbled such a hump, in tiny bites, chewing with care, one was rewarded with marvelous dreams of the future. The baker, enjoying a brisk trade, made a special offer to those wishing to limit their intake of sugar. He would sell them a single hump for double the price of a whole dwarf.

Trading his last coin and two flattering odes to the baker's plump wife, Cornelius filled his tattered pockets with sugar humps, and set off again on his journey.

The very next town he passed claimed to be the birthplace of the lady Morgantina. Of course there were the usual discrepancies about the circumstances of that celebrated birth, for in those days a really fine dwarf was often not born but made—and any greedy family who had the secret of dwarf-making could thereby earn a tidy misfortune. The queen's favorite, it was said, had once been merely an ordinary tiny babe, made to sleep in a tinder box inside her father's shoe, arms and legs folded crosswise and snugly fastened with strips of spotted catskin. Every night her mother rubbed the babe's perfectly formed limbs with a rare nut-colored substance named for a beautiful marquise who was the last woman of the town burned at the stake for witchcraft. There had been great rejoicing on Morgantina's first birthday, when a hideous little hump was seen to form on her left shoulder, and again the following night, when she was heard to utter her first dreadful word. Some said the word was "Merlin," and others insisted it was "Morgan le Fay." A gossip or two whispered that there had never been a hump at all, and that the infant's first word was merely "Mama," but Cornelius Agrippa, learned historian that he was, saw at once that the wisest course was to discount envious calumny, for by now the queen's dwarf was thought to be a treasure of the kingdom, and fools from many lands paid princely sums for any object that bore her likeness or her touch.

Throughout the countryside, humble citizens had taken Morgantina to their hearts. It was a time when there was everywhere a love of the frightfully marvelous, a delight in feeling afraid. Like the queen herself, every simple rustic might indulge in the enjoyment of an unseemly pleasure, a perverse vanity. The more dreadful a monster, the greater pride one must take in it. Such hideousness! Mistress and slave arrayed themselves in matching pride. Not being a frisk of nature, but possessing one; thus, owning a super-natural power.

In such a time, the monster itself needed only to be safely caged. Wealth, fame and perfect safety would follow; a golden thimble of life, filled with magnificent wine.

How cruel fate was, thought poor, learned Cornelius, with a pang of purest hate, as his weary feet carried him along life's dusty road. If only I were stunted and crookbacked; if only I had an idiot's grin and a misshapen child's body to cover my ambitions. For Cornelius was a handsome, strapping fellow, and he had not been fed a dainty morsel from a golden plate in a very long time.

By evening of the fifth day of his journey, Cornelius' heart lifted; before him rose a cluster of iridescent spires piercing the darkening sky like the peaks of highborn ladies' hats, or a nest of rare, hungry birds. How can it be? Cornelius thought. These were the turrets that had haunted all the stories of his childhood. He had dreamed a thousand dreams of a life within these walls; of dogs fighting beneath painted tables, jeweled monkeys scampering up silken draperies, of parrots shrieking a fierce blur of foreign curses in tongues of blue and green and flame. In the deep recesses of curving windows, curving marble benches had gleamed and beckoned him. Beneath the arrow slits, treasures of gold and silver had lain in careless heaps on carved pedestals, inviting the casual touch of his cool fingers. And, ah, had he not dreamed a flock of laughing courtesans, sporting naked upon the shining floors? He could imagine them even now, tumbling merrily beneath lighted candelabra; princes and cardinals in costly robes, white ringed hands darting like birds, tossing chestnuts for the maidens to chase. Cornelius himself would award the prize for the most impudent immodesty. What pretty writhing such women would perform for a sweetmeat, if it were followed by a silk petticoat or a pair of ribboned shoes. What sly jokes and compliments would be served then, with a supper of forty courses that would last till daybreak. He could taste their sausages on his parched tongue; venison and veal cooked together, and great slabs of fishes with silver scales, and roasted peacocks served whole in their feathers. He could see ladies with their shining hair caught in golden nets and glowing with pearls. He could hear famous poets whispering in awe and envy as Cornelius raised his beautiful voice in song. The praises he would sing them; the wonders he would conjure before them; the prophecies he would weave of the threads of their own wishes and rumors, and his hunger, and the world's will to believe.

CATHERINE WAS WEARING a scowl that made her skin turn the color of bruises. Not only was Morgantina sprawled like a poisonous insect in her doll's bed, nursing her foolish tongue, but the king had chosen this day to announce a piece of evil news. It was, to be sure, an announcement she had been dreading every day of her life with Henry, seven years of such days. Catherine, he had said, in a tone of pleasantry, the lady Diane will be coming to stay. Here? Catherine stammered. Here? Henry smiled like one with a slight headache. It will be better for us all, he had said, wearily. Something must be done, you know. The last he had said in a tone of reproach. Her fault, about not having an heir. Seven years of fault. And now the lady Diane. Here.

Henry waved a dismissive hand then, limp, glittering with his rings. And she'll help with the garden, he murmured. You know, she's got a glorious garden. All white, this spring, have you heard? And the red-and-blue one was stunning last year. One never thought she'd equal it.

She's not touching my garden, said Catherine.

Henry sighed. As you like, my dear. We'll let her have a plot to herself, then. Come, you shall choose it. He drew Catherine to the east window. There? he gestured.

No, she pouted. Over there. She pointed. I don't want to have to see it from my studio. Or my bedchamber. Or the hall, either. Henry, *why* must she come to stay?

He sighed again. I am nearly thirty, Catherine. Too old for riding through the chill night. He chuckled then, patting her gingerly as one does a sulky horse. You'll see, Catherine. The two of you will be friends. In a month you'll tell me you can't imagine life without her. Even that dwarf of yours will adore her.

She will not, snapped the queen. Morgantina adores no one unless I threaten her.

Henry smiled his headache smile again. Then you must remember to threaten her severely.

Catherine made her eyes blaze, but carefully folded her lips into a thin, silent line. Henry saw the two signs of defiance and opened his eyes to a question. Was there a further thing she wished to say?

I was curious, Catherine began, timidly. Whether she ... how long you ...

Why, as long as we live, Henry said. She has consented to accept our small gift, you see. The white house just across the river. In fact, she will widen the stream there, and build a splendid bridge of seven arches, so that our houses may connect. A covered walkway ... I think it will be a fine addition, don't you agree? And the walkway will be our new banquet hall.

Catherine inclined her head, or bowed it. Otherwise he would have seen the splotches of anger on her sallow cheeks. There were no tears. Catherine had no tears.

Shall we go in to our guests, then, little Catherine? He bent his arm. She lifted her white sleeve.

The lady Diane stood waiting, her black-and-silver gown gleaming like night, just inside the archway of the great feasting hall. Smiling, she stepped lightly between them, proffering a black winged arm to each. I am very happy, my queen, she whispered. Indeed, she had never looked more radiant. Catherine's eyes narrowed like a cat's, studying her. Did she truly bathe in asses' milk? Did she rub snail oil into her skin to make such a gleam? None who gazed upon them could have guessed the queen to be less than half her rival's age, or the king young enough to be his mistress' son. And none could mistake the king's pleasure in this moment, or which lady inspired it. Diane, he said, breathing it low as a word of song.

That was how the lady Diane came to live at court, as the queen's lady-in-waiting, and how the little stream that divided the royal grounds grew so wide that it flowed to the majestic breadth of seven graceful arches. That was how the lovely white house upon the opposite bank sprouted wings at its sides and grew as large as a palace. That was how there came to be, just opposite the queen's glowing

15

red-and-purple garden, another garden pale as the colors of the moon, of such tender beauty, such haunting night fragrance, that all who saw it spoke of it in a whisper, as though its charm were magical.

In the days to come, a great corridor would rise above the river bridge, with open archways echoing those of the bridge itself, forging a long, shapely link between the upper chambers of the lady Diane's house and those of the palace itself. Catherine and her dwarf Morgantina would be seen to pace restlessly along the great expanse of this corridor, measuring the shining diamonds of white and black stone. Their figures would dart in and out of the arches like bright threads, drawing stitches. Catherine raging and weeping, the dwarf uttering short, fierce whispers, as her tiny slippers raced behind the stamping feet of her queen. Yet we have need of Diane, Morgantina would cry one day, stopping sudden and breathless as a statue. Catherine would stare at the dwarf as though her look could dissolve the creature into a mound of quicklime. Need . . . of Diane! The echo would ring out over the polished stone diamonds, like prophecy, or a demon's call to harms.

HENRY SAT DRAWING in his drawing room. Over and over he sketched the same device; it was Diane's bold design for his new heraldic emblem. A great sturdy *H*, its two massive legs planted wide as the trunks of strong oak trees, embraced by a pair of graceful twining arms, all in leaf. At first glance these vines curved themselves into twin *C*'s, for Catherine forward and reverse. At the same time, these leafy arms formed a lovely pair of *D*'s, since a *C* embracing *H* must turn to a *D*, whether it will or no. *D* for Diane, then. Or perhaps *C* pressing *H* into the embrace of *D*, or *D* for her part drawing *H* tenderly from *C*. Or, again, *C* merely clinging sweetly to *H*, while *D* joined with them as one. Yet the whole made such an elegant, simple, proper form; Henry could have it blazoned everywhere without setting a single evil tongue in motion. Embedded in marble floors, carved in elaborate wood mantels, in lintels, in the shrubs of the queen's formal garden; embroidered in golden thread for the canopy over Catherine's bed. He would have it woven in the patterned cushions upon which they sat, side by side, receiving emissaries from Catherine's own country. Stamped in gold metal for the buckles of her footmen's codpieces. Henry smiled.

How like Diane this emblem was—at once bold and forthright, yet delicious in its sly wit. Henry sighed a great sigh of his pleasure. Was it not a fine thing to be a king, still young, his beard scant, with a slender trunk and a voice too high for commanding, yet with a mistress like this for his lifelong love; a Titania more beautiful than any, though past her fiftieth year. Did she thrive, as the gossips said, on mysterious tisanes? Had she blanched her skin with virgin's milk? Did virgins give milk? Was her hair blackened with devil's herbs or the hearts of ravens? He cared not. As for his sallow, sorrowful queen, his grave and silent suffering Catherine, she seemed to have sworn a maiden's vow, never to give pleasure nor take it in this life, save for the vicious games she played with the dwarf Morgantina. Henry could scarcely bear to visit his wife's chamber; until last night, he had stayed away nearly a full year since the seventh anniversary of their wedding. It would no longer do. Again it was Diane

17

who made him see both folly and wisdom, and the way between them. Somehow an heir must be got. In the end only Diane could devise the cure. She had moved to him and, in moving, moved them all.

For last night, the king had lain in Diane's arms, murmuring Mama . . . Mama, as he always did in the moments of his weakness. The dwarf Morgantina had waited just outside the door, under the crimson velvet hangings, with her tiny ear pressed to the yellow crack of light. Go to her now, Henry, whispered Diane. You shall get a fine son upon her at last. And he will be ours. And so it happened that Henry rose from the sweet musk of Diane's rose-colored bed, carried his passion away through the fragrant night garden, and scaled the stairs, two at a stride, to the cool white bedchamber of his sleeping wife. Catherine, he said, sounding her name like a cry of triumph. She yielded to him without a sound, and only Morgantina, now rolled into a ball in her accustomed hiding place inside the queen's great tasseled pillow, grimaced with her mistress' pain.

When Henry woke and took his leave, Catherine closed her parted thighs like the halves of a bitten fruit, and the dwarf wept loyally through her prayers. May Heaven grant . . . may Heaven spare . . .

You are a lucky dwarf, whispered the queen. I shall have him take you instead, the next time.

Morgantina trembled convincingly. I beg your pardon, my queen, she said. Not that I would die of it, but of the child. A child of the least ordinary size would rend me.

And good riddance, said the queen. Not that children come when you want them. They are very like dwarfs, in that respect.

Only uglier, said Morgantina.

18

THE LADY DIANE WOKE when a narrow wand of sunlight struck her pillow; it moved through her shining hair like the touch of a lover. She smiled, with her eyes still closed, stretching out her hand. I am here, she murmured. Then she sprang from the bed and ran barefooted to the window, flinging curtains aside to admit the silken breeze.

White moon-flowers fluttered wanly beneath the balcony, bowed under their morning weight like the heads of sullen children. Oh, but I thought it would all be pink, she sighed, and then clasped her impatient hands. She would have it all pink—at once. She would raise an army of the queen's gardeners to rout every pallid blossom. Slay the snapdragons, the irises, the lilies. By sundown she would have a rose tapestry spread like a feasting cloth. Peach flax unfolding to the riverbank, feathered fringes of love-in-a-mist, long-legged tulips the color of flesh. Roses, lustrous as Oriental pearls, blushing a hundred new echoes of their name. Henry adored Diane in pink. She never wore it.

CATHERINE MOVED CAUTIOUSLY in her rumpled cocoon of bedclothes, stained with the night's juices. Her thin nose quivered with distaste. Still, Henry had been kind. Had touched her as though her skin were not hateful. Sweet, he had whispered, once. Oh, sweet. As though for a moment she were not Catherine. As though, under his hand, her body had been transformed for a moment—made lush, rose-colored, wicked.

She had learned to harden her mind against such thoughts; she would make her small eyes dark and round with anger; she would roll over, tightening the tangle of soiled covers until they bound her like an ancient corpse in a winding sheet.

Morgantina read the queen's thoughts, smiling. Your husband, she said, wore a face of pleasure when he woke. Yet the lady Diane spent a sleepless night. I paid her a visit and counted her tears. There were fifty.

Catherine said nothing to this. With a laugh of mischief the dwarf unrolled herself from the fat tasseled pillow and slid to the floor. A fierce clattering could be heard from the gardens. Morgantina scuttered to the window and stood transfixed.

What is it? Catherine demanded.

Thieves, said Morgantina. Digging a thousand graves beneath the lady's chamber.

The queen propped herself on an elbow. Her garden?

Gone, said Morgantina. Pouf!

But what can it mean!

The dwarf shrugged her tiny shoulders so that her hump shook with authority. The lady has lost the king's attention. She must astonish us at once. Look there—she is merely turning a sea of white into one of rose. A fool's magic. The dwarf could not conceal the note of admiration in her voice. In truth, she hardly tried.

CORNELIUS THE STARGAZER, itinerant peddler of doubtful wonders, had requested an audience with the king. I cannot see him, Henry shouted, panic seizing his throat. Where was the lady Diane? He pulled twice at the cord beside his drawing table. Footmen flew like startled birds through the corridors in search of the king's mistress. She was out, gardening. Striding between beds of frangipani, magnolia, swimming in carnation. She must come at once. Tucking a stray moist tendril under the fine silver net that held the black curtain of her hair. Raising her whispering skirts, hurrying; hurrying to be at his side. Henry held his breath, counting her footsteps, counting the blows of his own heart. Diane; Diane.

My king, she murmured. I am with you. Her voice spread through his body like a healing tonic, a spirit perfume. Beads of sweat cooled upon Henry's brow as though she had touched him. The necromancer, he said. Must I see him?

What have we to fear from a peddler of easy mysteries? said Diane. Catherine has summoned him; he wants a job; we shall let her engage him. Or . . . not.

The dwarf—? said Henry.

The dwarf is ours.

She watches us—

As we watch her. Diane smiled and reached toward him. Long curling fingers light as smoke, cooling his mind as they warmed his skin. Her hand unfolded against him like a gift. Will it not amuse us to see him for a moment? And then I have a surprise for you.

Yes. Yes. Two bright spots of color inflamed Henry's cheeks. His eyes were bright with a fever of dread. Send him in.

Diane inclined her head to the guards; so slight a motion. Henry marveled at the speed with which the men leapt at her command; never doubting, not with a twist of the mouth or a flicker of eye. Like the mechanical toys he had loved as a boy; they obeyed; they marched; they killed and were killed in return, to be replaced by others exactly the same. He sighed with comfort; the fever spots faded from his cheeks.

The necromancer entered, bowing with a sweep of plumed hat; a ragged sweep, but pretty. Your Majesty's kindness, he murmured. I have come—

Does he paint portraits to the life? the king whispered to Diane. Diane whispered to her equerry, and so on down the line of courtiers. The last man cleared his throat. His Majesty wishes to know whether the learned master paints portraits. To the life.

Cornelius stared at Diane. I have rendered the ladies of the Gonzaga, the Marquise d'Aumont—

Has he ever done a naked dwarf? whispered Henry, licking his dry lips. Diane sent the whisper. Again the last courtier spoke. Ever done a naked dwarf?

Cornelius drew a breath. Once, he said. For the Duke Cosimo, his favorite Morgante. Naked, full-length, on both sides of the canvas. Front view on one side, back view on the reverse, and each with the same monstrous limbs and grotesque, repulsive body, the swollen belly, and the humpback that Morgante was possessed of. The magician paused, to lower his eyes in modesty. In its way, he added then, the picture was thought very fine, and praiseworthy.

O, Morgante, sighed Diane. Another pygmy named in jest for a tiresome giant. Not even a real giant.

The joke is badly worn, the king agreed, aloud. Then he whispered again to Diane. Does he do spectacles? Diane dispatched the royal question. Spectacles?

Once, said Cornelius again, with his modest bow, allowing his gaze to rest for a moment on the lady Diane. For Alfonse d'Este, a ballet with a dance of swords, performed by the Swiss Guards. He looked quickly at the king; Diane gave a nod of polite boredom. And then— Cornelius gestured grandly—I caused a great golden ball to descend, as from the heavens, only to melt away in a rosy burst of air; a sunrise. Four Virtues appeared on a blue sphere of smoke, singing. Of course we had freaks to represent the Vices. The clouds were made to form human faces. Glowing rocks . . . a volcanic eruption. Here Cornelius paused, as if for breath. Many who saw it swore that it gave . . . a vision into the depths of the human spirit. The magician lowered his eyes once more, and fell silent.

Diane whispered to the king. The king nodded, concealing his excitement. We have heard of it, he said.

Diane, whispering again, ticked off the major points on her slender fingers. Each courtier counted his fingers in turn. Again the last spoke. You will receive lodging, food, a suit of rich brocade. You will accept no other commissions. You will have charge of all festal decorations, both indoors and out. You will paint scenery and devise costumes for the court and their Majesties. All will be on a gigantic scale, more extraordinary than anything you have described.

Henry leaned forward and whispered directly to the courtier. The courtier cleared his throat. Astrological readings for his Majesty and the lady Diane. Portraits for the decoration of the lady Diane's private salon. As well as the queen's studio.

Mount Parnassus? said Cornelius. The Muses renouncing Mars' union with Venus?

Diane shook her head, whispering furiously.

Minerva expelling the Vices from the grove of Virtue?

Diana the huntress, said the courtier brusquely. Diana

---

and Minerva chasing satyrs. Classical attire for the queen. The lady Diane will sit for the portrait of her namesake.

And the queen? said Cornelius, boldly. For Minerva?

The king now shook his head. Diane whispered. Well, said the king aloud. We shall see if she would like it.

We will sit, said Diane, on different days.

If it please your Majesty, my lady, Cornelius ventured, My gifts as a portraitist are modest; I practice livelier arts. I must have supplies for my laboratory. Rare texts for my scholarly research. I must have a planisphere. An astrolabe. I am a theologian by training, a scholar by temperament. I—

The king's hand waved him to silence. Another exchange of whispers. The courtier spoke again. The lady Morgantina is also blessed with these gifts. You may share her library, if she permits. You are to read her palm tonight? Cornelius nodded. But if it please—

Good, said Diane. Then we shall all see how it goes.

Leave us now, said the king.

As Cornelius withdrew, Henry turned to Diane. What do we know about him?

He was at Metz, said Diane. Friend of that rogue Jacques the Bookseller. Whose ears they cut off.

Ah, said Henry, smiling. And then his nose?

And then his right hand, said Diane.

Henry sighed. At last—

—he was burned alive.

Henry made a noise of distaste, or sympathy. Life is hard for a young scholar with wit or conscience burning in him.

Mm, said Diane pleasantly. Court life is hard too. For an artist, a magician, a heretic, a necromancer—with guile and ambition burning in him.

24

Well, said Henry. We need no more scandal here—

And we shall have none. Diane twined her arm through his. Catherine will conceive; a chorus of rejoicing will drown the gossip.

That dwarf, though, said Henry. What if she seduces him?

Diane shook her head. His power and hers—compared to mine, my darling Henry? Let us not put our fear in small devils. It will poison us sooner than they would.

A footman appeared at the doorway. The queen begs permission, Majesty.

Diane's eyes flickered for an instant. I shall withdraw—

No, stay. The king's hand plucked at her sleeve; not a kingly gesture.

Henry, she said, making her voice soft. It is not wise— already Cornelius has a piece of news for her. It was she who summoned him.

Go, then. Henry released his grasp.

Catherine swept in, her skirts sighing about her ankles like ghostly secrets. She wore a chalk-white gown, heavy with seed pearls and shiny as a great festal cake. In it she seemed to struggle for air, pitching forward with each step, as though she were falling. Morgantina, jeweled and coiffed, clung to her mistress' train like a resplendent monkey. Her costume was identical to the queen's, even to the padded cap shaped like a plump white heart, which made her monstrous head even larger.

The magician? Catherine began. Cornelius was given leave to address your Majesty? Her tone was an accusation.

Yes, said Henry, gazing fiercely at his queen and her grotesque pet, who hung from her gown like a human

25

pendant. We have engaged him, Henry went on, as was your wish, my dear. Are you well pleased, Catherine?

The queen stared down at the points of her shoes; they peered from beneath her gown like spies. Well pleased, my lord. Only—

Only?

Catherine's voice was now plaintive, a thin whine. You didn't ask what I wanted of him. You gave him a hundred tasks that are nothing to do with me. And I wished—

You wished?

My stars. I wished for a telling of my stars, every day. And of Morgantina's—

Henry drew his brows together and lowered his head, raising his shoulders to affect a look of fierceness. Sparse brows they were, and padded shoulders, but the effect was scowl enough for Catherine. Foolishness, Henry growled. My court requires no gypsy ravings. Conjurers' lies, charms, tricks. You have your dwarf; what more need have you of fools' wisdom?

But— Catherine bit her mouth into silence.

In any case, you had no right to summon this man. Henry folded his arms, as Diane had taught him; planting his feet apart until he felt himself grow larger. This . . . vagrant rogue, he went on. A . . . dabbler in black mischiefs. I have given him honest work to do, which may stay the tongues of my enemies—now that you have set them in motion. He says he can paint; we shall have him try a portrait of you. Can't be worse than the last one. As for Morgantina, he shall try to paint her too. We'll inscribe her on a medallion. Send it to the Orient, perhaps. Get you a bolt of embroidered silk for another pair of splendid gowns like those. Will she like that? What color would she like? Eh?

Morgantina had been burrowing steadily into the folds of Catherine's skirt. By now she was all but invisible. I thank you, Majesty, she said, in a voice that seemed to come from elsewhere. She blended so well into the thick white nimbus surrounding the queen that nothing of her form remained apart, save for the minuscule feather parasol she carried; it trailed behind her now on the crimson carpet, like the tail of a ragged bird. Yet half hidden as she was, her gaze was bold; it caught the king's eye with a stare so intense that he felt himself seized. Cold trickles of royal sweat sprouted upon the royal torso, and crept stealthily down. The dwarf's look was a challenge; a dare. As if she reproached Henry for her deformity, for her size, for her station—or for his. Henry shuddered and lowered his gaze, as a king must never do.

CORNELIUS FOUND A GOOD SUPPER in his room: roasted pigeon, rough bread, and wine the color of royal blood. Tucked inside a silver fruit bowl was a rare text of witch trials, recounting the notorious events at Saint Pé, wherein twenty maidens swore that each had given herself to the devil, and each was examined by judges, who found them all to be maidens still. Nevertheless all twenty were burned forthwith, some, as witnesses said, seeming to be in a great hurry. As always, the inquisitors preferred the confession to the fact.

In the mighty forest . . . whispered a sudden voice from beneath the table where Cornelius sat. In the mighty forest, the women became wolves and devoured the passersby—even when none had passed by.

I know who is there, said Cornelius with studied calm, and popped a plump green fig into his mouth. For of course it was the dwarf. She sprang out with an imp's laugh, whirling a cloak of scarlet satin. In the candlelight she shone and flickered like the wine in his goblet, a dancing flame. Good evening, Sir Magician, she said, arranging a smile that might imply promises. Cornelius did not smile back, but raised his glass to her. Have you come for an early glimpse into your future, milady?

Certainly not, said the dwarf. I have come to give you false clues. Useful ones, of course. I have heard you are a hopeless necromantic.

I have heard you play with words, said Cornelius. But very well. Give me such a clue as you will.

I am thinking of it; you must divine it. And if you cannot divine it, then I will devil it. Morgantina leapt up onto the table, spreading her cloak about her like a circle of fire. She helped herself to a morsel of bread, digging it out of the center of the loaf with both tiny fists. When she had plucked what she wanted, she kneaded it with thumb and finger into the shape of a rough pearl, held it up to the light, turning it this way and that, until she was satisfied. Then she gobbled it down, in three precise bites.

Some wine? Cornelius asked pleasantly.

She nodded her head and held out the tiny crystal thimble which she wore around her neck on a long chain of fine gold. He filled the thimble; she drained it; he filled it again. When she had emptied it a third time, she turned it upside down, and it vanished in the folds of her cloak.

Now, she said.

You will take a long journey in a blackberry pie, he began. When the pie is opened, you will pop out, richly adorned with precious jewels and splotched here and there with berry stains in the shape of wolves. People will gasp in amazement.

Morgantina's mouth dropped open in a tiny yawn. I do that all the time, she said. Twice a year I have to take a pie trip to the queen's sister in the north of Italy, or her cousin in the south of Spain. They send their dwarfs to Catherine; everyone likes a change. Unless there is a plague, or someone threatens to marry me off to one of their monsters. A few of them would have us bred, you know, like dogs.

Terrible, murmured Cornelius, trying for a sincere tone. He could not stop staring at her. She had a way of hooding her eyes suddenly, or retracting her upper lip in a snarl, while the rest of her face bore the most ordinary expression.

She caught him studying her. What would you like to do with me? she said softly. It was less a question than a charge. She stood up, abruptly, on the table, so that her eyes were level with his. He saw that the eyes had too many colors, like the sharp bits of glass in a spectrologist's prism. I would like—he stammered.

She laughed. You would like to profit from knowing me. To travel from one court to the next telling marvelous stories of me. To paint my portrait, nude, festooned with grapes like a baby Bacchus. Of course, you'll never get a decent likeness. They never do. But you'll carry it about, to illustrate your amusing chat. You'll tell them that I ... and that I ... am I right, Sir Magician? Or no?

I would like ... he whispered hoarsely. I would like to see—

Morgantina laughed again, and flung her cape up over her head. She stood naked before him, her tiny stunted limbs glistening in the firelight. Do I please you? she said.

29

Her voice, muffled by the crimson cloth, had an eerie sound, like the cry of someone strangling in darkness.

Please, said Cornelius. He found it difficult to breathe.

The dwarf began to whirl in a slow pirouette, so that the cloak, released, flared out like a discus in flight. The hem of it overturned the wine and caught the edge of a candle flame. Cornelius could make no move; not to rescue the precious goblet or the tray of scattering food. He sat as though rooted, gazing at this demonic figure, beating out flames with her satin finery, with her fists, her bare little feet. He fought an impulse to reach out and touch her flesh, for he could not decide whether to strike or caress it. For God's sake, cover yourself! he cried at last, raising an unsteady hand to his own face. He felt himself burning with a shameful heat.

She let the charred cloak drop around her. As you like, she said, bending close to study him. He shrank from her as if in fear for his life. You need never reveal more than you dare, Cornelius, she said. But you have not sifted my false clues.

Enough, said Cornelius, mustering his dignity. I will save my words for the queen's ears. Or else the king's.

Aha! Morgantina waggled a finger under his nose. You want to stay? You need a patron? Willing to spend your days in the queen's bedchamber, reading ladies' horoscopes? "Tomorrow you will be bored; beware of Thursday—boredom will come to you from afar." Will you spy upon the lady Diane? Will you serve as jester when I am gone to Italy in my pie? Can you juggle? And at night—will you creep into my library to pursue your unholy . . . studies? Or—the dwarf drew a breath—is it merely that you have fallen in love with a monster?

Cornelius only shook his head.

30

O, I forgot, added Morgantina, now with a look of pity. The king has sent for you. The lady Diane wishes to be entertained. Be careful, won't you?

LATER, IN THE QUEEN'S RED SALON, Cornelius frowned at the dwarf's upturned palm, turning it this way and that. The lines were delicate as veins of a pale leaf, intricate as strands of an insect's web. The magician's lips moved as though to commit each line to memory, before deciphering its encoded message. There has been much pain in the lady's past, he began, like any trifler. The queen, pretending to look on with interest, suddenly thrust her golden darning needle deep into Morgantina's side. The dwarf uttered a piercing shriek. Much pain, murmured the queen, smiling. In the past, you say? How fascinating.

Cornelius tried again. I see a great hall of glass, many admirers, someone singing . . . Here is feasting, a table filled with rare delights. The lady has a bright object in her hand; she attacks her supper with it; a slender silver stick—no, a dagger with three points; a tiny trident.

Catherine started. In my father's kingdom, she murmured, we cut our meat with the fork.

A fork! exclaimed Cornelius, marveling. Morgantina will introduce this custom at your court.

Catherine looked doubtful. We will be ridiculed. It will be said we are fools. That I am of a race of freaks. Like her.

It is in my palm, said Morgantina.

Cornelius nodded. No mistaking it.

31

Go on, said Catherine.

Here is a child's cradle, said the magician. Morgantina pulled her hand away as though he had burned it.

Ha! said the queen, wagging a finger.

The infant's gown bears the royal monogram, said the magician. Each word fell slowly from his lips, as though the effort to speak it cost him dearly.

He lies! The dwarf's face twisted in fear. There is no child.

Cornelius smiled. No child of yours, my lady, but the queen's. How else would it wear the monogram?

But why is it here? pleaded the dwarf, rubbing at the spot he indicated, as though to erase it. In *my* hand? Cornelius spoke in a soothing voice. You will watch over the babe, will you not? For there are shadows about. See, here? And here another—

Is it Diane? whispered Catherine. Let me see—

I cannot tell that, said Cornelius, with a great solemnity.

Morgantina stamped her foot, making the sound of a powder puff on glass. What is any of it to do with me? Can you not see anything of *me*?

I see—Cornelius began, then shook his head. No—that is all.

Morgantina saw that his lips paled. All dwarfs die young, she said, in a tone of ice. Then she withdrew her hand.

The queen yawned. Let us play another game, magician, if you know one. Can you conjure a killing frost tonight? One that destroys only pink blossoms, while yellow and crimson thrive? Can you make a quiet stream overflow its banks, so that the stones of a new bridge give way—so that all plunge with a terrible crash into the water? Or—wait—can you, could you—

Morgantina laughed. I know! Could you crumple the face of a beauty while she bathes tonight in virgin's tears?

Cornelius smiled. I can do none of those things, Majesty. But the queen does not require that they be done. And that is my good fortune.

Indeed, said Catherine. Then what use are you to us?

I confess I do not yet know. But this I swear: the queen will be glad of my service.

What about the dwarf? said Morgantina.

The magician bowed. One dare not presume to foretell a lady's fortune twice in a day.

Another answer that answers not! cried the dwarf. Again she stamped her foot; again her soft shoe made no sound upon the shining floor. A dwarf's anger is a thing of no consequence.

When he had gone, Catherine pinched Morgantina, and scolded her for Cornelius' reading. Then she asked, with a sudden coyness, Will you make him love me?

Perhaps, said the dwarf.

Morgantina hopped upon her mistress' table and swung her bandy legs back and forth. Humming, she plunged one finger into a bottle of violet water, another into one of green. She sniffed each finger delicately, then traced her name in perfume upon the glass tabletop. She spilled pink and yellow powders; she blew and swirled them into fanciful patterns. When the magician plays our game of who can tell, she said, all the endings will be a surprise.

O, you never make anyone love me, said Catherine. You don't really care about me at all. My sister is right; a dwarf cannot have feelings, it is not a person after all. She is right to keep hers in cages. And never let them come to her parties. You are worse than a monkey, even if you don't foul your clothes. It is said that the Este beat and starve their creatures. Percheo has to beg for morsels

33

under the table; one kicks him away. You are spoiled. You—

Actually, said Morgantina, Beatrice is kinder than you are. Often she comes to the dwarf house and plays with us all for an hour, as a child plays with dolls. She hardly ever pinches. We have tea and little cakes; she dresses us up and down, and combs our hair, and tucks us into little beds. And when I was there last, we had a lovely wedding. A real one. Twenty tiny couples, all bedecked in pearls and white taffeties. After we supped she had us undress, and the servants painted us gold all over. We were made to stand naked in the birdbaths, posed as bacchantes. The guests threw sweetmeats and coins. We dove. Only one drowned.

As she listened, Catherine grew silent, then excited. We could have a party like that! Beatrice would lend us a few of her creatures, wouldn't she? I could send a pair of peacocks in exchange. Or the new chimpanzees. God knows she is always borrowing my things. Last year she let several die. She is so careless.

We shall see, said Morgantina, who had invented the whole story. Meanwhile, it would be a fine thing if Cornelius planned a feast of magic with that golden fire he boasted of, and the puffs of orange smoke.

I could wear my blood-red jewels, mused Catherine.

I could mutter my imprecations, said Morgantina.

Mm. But what will Diane do?

O, she will wear black as always. Morgantina's smile was a mischief. She does look splendid in black, though.

It's disgusting, said Catherine. Mourning, indeed. For that ancient pudding that Henry married her off to. For my sake, he said. It is always for my sake. As if I cared whether he had a widowed whore instead of a plain one.

Peace, my queen, said Morgantina. It does not do to excite yourself after a night of love. The baby will curdle.

Love? snapped the queen. From her sheets to mine? Do you imagine I am not ashamed?

What shame if it gets an heir? Morgantina shrugged her good shoulder.

What shame! Even you mock me. I swear I shall set him on you tonight. The monster you get shall wear his cursed monogram. And you shall die like the toad you are, split in twain to birth it! Now leave me. Leave me alone!

Morgantina sat perfectly still, slumped over her feet, which she thrust straight out before her, giving her the look of a rag puppet. I beg you, she cried, tear me apart some other way. Use the saw, or the pincers.

Ha! said the queen. Well I know how to repay a monster for its monstrosity. You *shall* bury Henry's sword tonight. He'll get his royal bastard—she poked the dwarf's belly—and when it comes you'll be halved as well as doubled. A good riddance to all.

Morgantina wept loudly, though the wellsprings of her true sorrow had dried in her long ago. Since neither a dwarf nor a queen sheds tears, one need never believe that either is human.

THAT NIGHT CORNELIUS emptied his pockets of magic sugar dwarf humps, and nibbled one in slow small bites. He was rewarded with three magnificent dreams. The first was of a garden of love, a small corner plot shaped exactly like Morgantina's hump, and planted with a succession of white flowers shining in the moonlight: hollyhocks, snow-in-summer. Morgantina sat in the shade of a tree filled with silver fruit, surrounded by a band of naked revelers. Wisps of gauze trailed and fluttered among the dancers' entwined limbs; their faces bore a look of transport; their lips glistened with wine, their flesh with sweet juices wrung from fruit or passion. The dwarf, hidden from them, was naked too. Her gaze swept past them to Cornelius, as though to purge him of delight in the scene. The dancing bodies were joyous to behold. Morgantina's twisted form, hunched like a question mark of flesh, mocked their beauty and cursed it. A moan of horror escaped Cornelius' lips; it was Morgantina he desired.

In the second dream, Cornelius saw himself arrayed in a suit of armor, kneeling at the foot of Henry's throne. Catherine stood towering above him, alone, wearing a gown of glittering black stuff that seemed to crackle with light. At her left side stood the lady Diane, pale and swooning. The dwarf Morgantina stood at the queen's right, half hidden by a cloak of iridescent feathers that rose and fluttered in a breeze that stirred nowhere else. The queen held aloft a great curving sword, its hilt ablaze with a single ruby, a bulging eye of blood. Defender of the Faith! Catherine said, laying the flat of her sword upon Cornelius' shoulder. A murderous echo rose up around them. Defender! Faith! One voice, higher than the rest, uttered a piercing shriek of pain, like the cry of a strangling bird. Then it spoke: Defend *me*! Let Faith fend for itself! Suddenly the dwarf seized the queen's naked curving blade and swung it sharply across the bowed neck of Cornelius; his fair head rolled smoothly, silently, to the white carpet, spewing a fountain of blood that spread its slow stain until all that was white had turned crimson. Catherine stepped lightly from her throne and placed one slender foot upon the neck of her fallen knight, lifting the hem of her robe safely above the pool of his blood. The feathered dwarf, in a sudden rustling of golden-green and violet-black, swooped and circled, dove and soared away.

In the final dream, Cornelius was in shackles, chained to the stone of a dungeon wall that gleamed wet with his own blood. His hand grasped a sharpened stick: he was writing a message in the dust. The devil has the fruit, he wrote. I have only the root. Yet it is the root of all I lost when I found it.

Cornelius of the dream then laid down his crude instrument and closed his eyes, so that he might indulge in a clearer vision. Behind the drawn shades of his own darkness, deeper than the darkness of his prison cave, yet another image appeared. In this dream within the third dream, another Cornelius appeared, dragging his broken chain, leaning upon the sharpened stick that served him now as both staff and weapon. He stood halfway up a steep mountain path, poised uncertainly in mist, balancing. The dwarf Morgantina, wearing a heavy robe of blazing white and the cowl of an abbess, stood before him. Do you pray for me? said Cornelius in the prisoner's dream. The dwarf shrugged her good shoulder. What you destroy may be your prayer. Then how will it be answered? he demanded. The dwarf-abbess replied, in a voice like cool water: There is no answer; the past suffers but cannot die. The dead are with you as you are with them. Cornelius the holy traveler opened his lips to reply; the dwarf vanished, leaving only an echo of unkind laughter that filled his eyes and mouth like sand.

MORGANTINA'S ROOMS, the dwarf apartments, were a scale model of the great palace itself. They were reached by an exquisite curving marble stair that spiraled downward from behind Catherine's private chapel. Catherine had worked with the court architect to fashion the low vaulted ceilings here, the archways and shadowed niches in which a dwarf might disappear for a game of hide-and-seek. To confound the vision, a dozen painted Morgantinas peeped from behind pillars, through half-open doorways, at the edges of curtained windows. Which were real? Which Morgantinas, which pillars and doors, which windows and arches? Did the breeze stir the drapery there, or was that an artist's trick? A trick of the light? Of the visitor's own darting eye? The walls glowed with miniature paintings and tapestries faithfully copied from the queen's own treasures. Plump little chairs sat about, in costly velvets and silks, under painted dwarfs in royal costume, who glared out from a tangle of apes and ermines, normal smiling children, and dogs as large as they.

Behind the tapestries, carefully hidden, were a hundred more secret paintings, telling other stories of dwarfs and masters, disguised as gods, satyrs, devils. These are the work of Morgantina, and they are never seen. What does a dwarf know of the nature of kings anyway?

Shall Cornelius steal them in the end? Must Morgantina destroy them herself? If necessary, will she paint her own face over all of theirs? When she is sold? burned? banished? When her tongue is cut off? Perhaps her works will be proclaimed a national treasure. Perhaps they will be called the Catherine paintings, later attributed to Cornelius Agrippa. When Diane is banished, when Henry is dead, when Cornelius' eyes are put out, and he is thrown into the dungeon? When Catherine takes to wearing black, identical to Diane; will the games of her salon, feasts, her

laughter, echo in the cropped ears of her former magician?
Will there be a new court favorite then? A set of dwarfs;
of princes?

THE QUEEN SAT in her red salon, surrounded by her
favorites: a poet smith, one of those who beat out verses
to order on their anvils, a writer of romance, a clever
gossip, a new humorist, and old Tito Strozzi, the court
poet, who now took to his pen only on solemn occasions—
the arrival of a foreign prince, a wedding, a great military
victory. Strozzi had once been excessively in love with a
charming singer, the young golden-haired Anthea, to whom
he had written a cycle of sonnets so passionate that they
had made him famous—and made her the object of an
obsessive lust in a duke and a cardinal's brother. The duke
had cut the throat of the cardinal's brother, and then paid
for his indiscretion with an eye and four fingers of the
right hand. Anthea grew old in a convent, under a vow
of silence. Strozzi, the poet who had caused it all, escaped
with his inflammatory sonnets; years later he presented
them and himself at the court of Catherine and Henry.
By then of course he had rededicated the sonnets many
times, to many noble ladies. Catherine was the last queen
in Europe who had not heard them. Strozzi had first been
engaged to instruct the little queen and her dwarf in the
art of turning verses. He was a private secretary now,
growing old in service. And not so beloved anymore. Hu-
miliating for a man like that to beg a woman for a new
shirt, to pay for it with an old sonnet. Still, a court poet
has free lodging and a florin a month to spend.
    Once, long ago in another land, Cornelius too had done

----

a piece of bold work, a series of beautiful sonnets dedicated, by an odd coincidence, to a girl named Anthea. But the time, the mood of the people, the particular golden glow of Cornelius, coming as he had from a distant place—feeding the hunger for simple goldenness in this dark and fanciful moment—all continued to conspire to give him fresh triumph. Of course he had begun by having earned it. The finest trick of a trickster is to deserve his first prize. The true love for Anthea became the useful love of Laura or Isabella or Lucrezia. One learned to alter the details, and the emotions, to suit. Now Cornelius must have his dwindling magic praised. It is a disappearing act: first a seduction, then an addiction, then a self-destruction. Soon it is only the praise that warms him; echoes of an ancient flame. Finally his gift is the echo itself. His art is become a sleight of hand.

So it was that Cornelius knew Strozzi's game well. He would play a different one. Melancholic, he would not go much to the salon. He would husband his brooding air, his shy and mysterious presence, his worldly sadness that challenged a lady to stir him.

But today he had been summoned: the fatal interview. He dressed with care. The green? Too flamboyant, perhaps. He must carry the air of a man who cared little for fine clothes; he must be a poet rumpled but not ragged. He must fling his cloak carelessly over one shoulder; wind a scarf about his throat; wear outdoor boots with a spatter of mud. He would come to them tousled and red-cheeked, his hair spangled with droplets of mist. A man who walked alone with his thoughts along the wilder edge of woods. Eager flatterers arrive early. Arrogant favorites arrive late. He would come at the moment summoned, flushed and blinking at the warm light. He would come armed

with the three discourses on love that he had read aloud
in Asolo at the court of the exiled queen of Cyprus. The
ink would appear still wet. Petrarchian! they would ex-
claim. Enough of pretty rhymes, here is a philosopher, an
artist of wisdoms. The queen would whisper to her dwarf;
the dwarf would whisper back.

The First Discourse

Cornelius reads: A lover's gifts. The first gift elicits
embarrassment, refusal, protestation, a jousting with
conscience—all covered with a pretty flush of guilty
pleasure.

The second gift brings delight unabashed. The
gift of pleasure through appreciation. The giver basks
in warmth. The beloved appreciates it; thus she appreciates me; I am exalted. The third gift is a turning
point. The beloved gives a trifle in return (clumsily
but with a full heart). She extends herself; she makes
a sacrifice. She lets the lover know she can ill afford
to make such gifts. He basks again; his beloved loves
in return.

At last, the habit of acceptance grows between
them. It is unadmitted; therefore it is not perceived
to be growing. Nor can the disparity ever again be
acknowledged, since it now must make the beloved
ashamed to receive, and the lover unkind to call attention. But the giving grows apace, and becomes a
great basic lie between them: that they give equally,
that they are equals, that the charming beloved gives
something of great and priceless value, while the
grateful lover feels that all he gives is dross; a jewel,

41

valuables. The greater gift is contemptible, is unmentionable. Who supports whom? They merely "love."

Now again, the habit becomes one of expectation and finally demand. The lover is become a victim of demand, but this too is never mentioned. In fact, the lover is guilty if the poor beloved is forced to ask for (beg for) what the lover once so freely gave. And he now grows uncomfortable, bitter, unloving. He begins to withhold, consciously, for the first time. He begins to count up his gifts, to weigh them against hers, which are intangible and therefore beyond price. She begins to give these grudgingly now, feeling (or saying she feels) ill-used; unloved.

Alas, poor beloved. She must begin to trade upon her lover's guilt, to exaggerate her needs. His gifts are no longer optional; they are debts. He owes it to her to pay and pay again for value received. There is no longer a question of love. Each has been or claims to have been betrayed, seduced, deceived. His gifts are discounted twice: once, because they were easy; the second time, because they were not freely bestowed. Her gifts remain precious, unique, incomparable. After all, they never could be measured. The gift of love, the bestowal of a smile, a caress. Her gaze which gave him life, which made him feel invincible. So long as he had her as his talisman, so long as he was in her power, he was his best, his truest self. Now he is less. The riddle: Who was the robber? What was the treasure? Love is. Love was.

The dwarf sits under the queen's chair painting the salonistes in classic poses—as dwarfs, fools, jesters. The

queen tosses morsels of food to her. She tosses jests back.
It is a game of catch, a trainer with his dog.

THE SECOND DISCOURSE

Cornelius reads: How the ugly becomes beautiful and
then ugly again, before our very eyes. I could never
love a lady who had too much fat, or a nobleman with
too little hair. Yet once I did in either case, and saw
no fat, and saw no shining pate. For the gift is shadow
play; love is not blind at all; it is only a steady gaze
shimmering in its own light. Does not the witch cast
a glamour before her own eyes? Perhaps my lady
love was slender, now I think of it. Perhaps the nobleman's hair was only fine, like a child's. The question is: When did that lady grow fat to my gaze?
when did the light begin its high dance upon that
nobleman's brow?

THE THIRD DISCOURSE

Cornelius reads: The artist cultivates his arrogance
more than his gift. They have taken me in, he cries;
why should they not? I give them my vision and my
laughter; I play their fool, their seer, their healer,
their wizard. They will never turn on me. They will
believe that their need of me is greater than mine of
them. That is the lesson I must teach them first. Their
need is greater because they are rich and empty,
while I am humble and full of life. Only let them
taste of me and they will come alive; they will drain

43

me if I let them. Which is the parasite, which the host? On which side is whose bread buttered?

Cornelius, flushed with his audacity, says: May I sit here, Majesty, on the floor with Morgantina? The others are charmed. Eyebrows lift. There are whispers of shock, a breeze of suspicion. What do we think? Catherine laughs, claps her hands. The rogue is not one who fawns. He does not reek of humility. Simply, he says: I prefer the view from below.

Strozzi is the first to applaud. He rises to his feet and bows. The art of survival, for a court poet (indeed for any privileged aging servant), is to read the signs first—to respond first. The fellow's discourses are old, Strozzi knows. He knows them by heart. Shall he denounce the fellow? No, one must bide one's time; make a friend. Time enough later for exposure, for scandal. First, perhaps, put the fellow in one's debt. Then in one's pocket. One can never tell when a good turn may be repaid, or how.

But another poet, young, upcoming, uncertain, a Strozzi protégé, struggles slowly to his feet, bewildered, tripping and tumbling into the fountain. His brocade—indeed, his future—ruined in an instant's merriment. Cornelius, gracious, proffers his cloak. The young man refuses, withdraws, dripping and shuddering, crimson with rage. He will be gone from the court within a fortnight. Strozzi will give him a lukewarm reference.

As Catherine rises to go, she pauses. How does the lady Diane's portrait go? As well, Cornelius says carefully, as can be expected.

We are leaving, Catherine says. A long journey. An urgent matter.

Cornelius bows. Does the lady Morgantina accompany you?

Not this time. Perhaps you may amuse each other.

The king has ordered a study of Morgantina. A medallion, perhaps?

Catherine frowns. Yes. Well. She holds out her hand. He bends to it. A safe return, madam.

CATHERINE LAY MOTIONLESS upon her bed, remembering the Italian dawn of her childhood, all rose and warm gold, so different from this weak pale light of the north. She had not slept all this night. What must she say to the Pope, her cousin, to pry loose those pearls that Henry craved? How could Henry charge her with such a task? And how could she fail him? In all these years no heir, and now, no support for his ventures. A sorry queen indeed.

Cornelius stood at the doorway. Madam. He spoke gently, almost in a whisper. I have cast the horoscope, but I should like to offer another gift. A healing gift for the difficult journey before you.

What gift? she demanded.

You will permit me to guide you? He stood now beside the bed and held out his right hand, not quite touching her. She felt her hair rise from the pillow as though a hot breeze stirred it. What—? she began again and then fell silent. Her eyes were heavy; the slender figure of Cornelius filled the vast space from where she lay to the great windows. The light now hurt her eyes; she closed them. She felt the man moving behind her, then beside her, speaking softly in a language she did not know. Suddenly he grasped her right foot and pressed it, his fingers a sharp vise; he held on as though waiting for a signal. She did not cry out, although the pain was everywhere in her body. He pressed again, harder now; she kept her silence. Perhaps he would kill her here, upon her silken bed? She knew that he would not. At last he released the foot and moved behind her, lifting her shoulders, holding them as though she were a child in a bath, as though she might sink and drown. Still she made no sound. Still he whispered—incantations, ancient prayers to profane gods, soothing promises to devils. The sounds came to her ear charged with light, shimmering like watered silk. He touched her limbs, he pressed each place according to some secret chart or plan, each time to the point of pain or laughter. An intimacy bordering on treason. She felt not the slightest fear, nor the slightest pleasure. Only his liquid voice pouring over her, his insistent words that had no meaning, yet held her prisoned. Yes, she thought. Yes to what? If he would not leave off speaking, touching, yes, she would consent to die or live.

Catherine, he was saying, in the foreigner's voice, but now her name, clearly her name. Catherine, he commanded. You will come back when you are ready. You will know what you need to know and the rest will pass through you. Again she felt his hands, motionless near her head, not touching, only hovering there like watchful birds. The air they stirred warmed her as though she stood close to a merry fire.

In an instant the warmth had vanished, and the voice. She opened her eyes to her great empty room, the slow pale dawn still rising. A dream? Morgantina! she cried. The dwarf lay tightly coiled inside the great tasseled pil-

low at her mistress' feet; she hugged six remarkable drawings of the queen entranced, of the magician Cornelius
touching the royal thighs in the cold silver light. She
stirred as though the queen's voice had wakened her. Majesty? she murmured, feigning a tiny yawn.

FROM THE GREAT ROUND WINDOW of her studio, Diane
watched her new bridge lifting its curved white arms to
the sun. Soon there would be a great banquet hall above
it, spanning the breadth of the river. Soon one might cross
directly from her house to the upper story of the castle,
heedless of inclement weather, the curious gaze of guards
in the courtyards, or visitors strolling in the gardens.
Every third square along that gleaming corridor would
bear the famous royal monogram, looming before the traveler's eye, reminding him that Henry, Catherine, and Diane were joined here in love or its likeness, forever.

Madam. A brace of guards, halberds crossed, an-
nounced the arrival of the new court painter. Diane turned,
smiling. The queen, he began, had reached a new decision
about her salon. Upon the ceiling, the goddesses Diana
and Minerva would give chase to the satyrs. Instead of
Minerva expelling the Vices.

Very well. Diane's own ceiling, then . . . She paused.
Had Cornelius been informed of how the last court painter
lost his position? Did he, Cornelius, understand that, like
the queen, Diane had certain ideas for the execution of
works in her studio?

He knew, of course. The finest masters of Europe vied
for the lady's invitations. It was known that any painter

she engaged might omit any detail from her designs, but that he might not add or change one.

Some there are who resist my rules, Diane said. They are not invited. In one case, a fellow stayed a full year, only to leave then, in despair. That one was dismissed by the queen, however. He had failed to capture a true likeness of the dwarf Morgantina. Though many, including Diane, had thought the piece quite arresting, in its way. It had been destroyed, of course, along with the artist's reputation.

Where was the fellow now? Cornelius asked. Diane's face was impassive. Dead, she believed.

Cornelius bowed. Very well, he said. Shall we begin?

The lady was wearing a simple cloak of silken velvet, so black that it drew all light to it, with no cast of blue or chestnut. It had a high collar that framed her white throat like a ring of night, ending in a clasp made of a single great emerald the size of a man's thumb. Shall I remove this? she said, as he gaped.

Cornelius shook his head. He would set up his easel. He would mix his colors. He would draw the draperies at the window to admit more light. She must stand just there, if she would. Where the light might fall in a stream toward her. Now—

She unfastened the clasp so that the velvet fell gently to the side. One breast lay revealed like a perfect rising moon against a night sky. Cornelius drew a breath in silence.

The king wishes, said the lady Diane.

The king wishes, he echoed. She had drawn the velvet panels farther apart, like curtains unfolding a drama.

If you would turn so, to the light, he said briskly.

She made a motion, deliberately the reverse. A test.

48

The light must strike me from this angle, she said. There. Look at the glass.

Cornelius frowned. No, madam. Forgive me; I think—

Her lips curled. Like this, then? Again she moved in another direction. He gestured. Just there—

She turned again. No. This is best.

For a quarter-hour they parried, each refusing the other's signal; neither giving way. Cornelius could not allow a hint of impatience in his tone. Diane condescended; was the man stupid?

If you are tired, he said finally, we could begin tomorrow. The light is going—

No, she said, pleasantly. We shall find a way to begin.

But we have, he replied. It is here. He gestured with a brush, dripping black.

What if I were to tell you, said Diane, that I know your blackest secret? Her teeth shone. Small, perfect teeth. A child's smile upon a face of fifty? Cornelius daubed the brush tip upon his canvas; his hand was steady.

You suffer, Diane went on, from a reasonable fear that if you fail here, you will have had the last of your chances.

As a dauber of paint, madam? He continued stroking the sooty brush. Whorls; crescents. He would not look at her.

As a dabbler in fortunes.

With respect, he said, there is always a place for a dabbler in fortunes.

Diane fell silent, appearing to consider this. Not always.

He glanced upward quickly, to see if she smiled. She did, but it was not a look of warmth or lightness. Diane smiled only with a lifting corner of her mouth. Some said she liked not the lines about her eyes that revealed themselves with a true laughter. Cornelius, studying her, saw at once that it was not for vanity at all that she withheld a woman's easiest gesture. Rather, it was this: a true smile might cost a moment's loss of clarity. As for tears, these posed the greater risk. The eyes, narrow and close, are misted over, fail to catch the details. The lady Diane controlled her eyes as all ladies, all performers, must. Pretend to express what others seek to feel. Cornelius knew the art as well, better than all his others. They were twins, he and she; he must allow her to discover it.

That is enough, she said suddenly. You shall destroy what you have done today. We may start again after you have begun work on the queen.

Cornelius' mouth opened, but no protest issued forth. Madam, he said. His brush rose as though to strike; he was unaware of it. Ah—he stammered. If one might beg the lady's indulgence. She paused at the doorway, but did not turn her head.

I have been giving thought to the lady Diane's salon, he said. Might she consider the color blue? Such rooms, as she knows, are always yellow. As the queen's studio—

Blue. Diane's nod was barely perceptible.

CATHERINE STOOD before her looking-glass, turning slowly to observe the line of her gown as its heavy folds moved with the light. The dwarf sat cross-legged at her feet. Cushions, bristling with pins, were strapped to each of her wrists, and a third lay bound tight about her head, like a crown of thorns.

Just there, said the queen, frowning. Another crystal rose. No, two more. And larger.

But—said Morgantina.

But?

It will make the gown too heavy. See—already it pulls to the side.

Catherine's foot shot forth like the tongue of a snake. The dwarf darted out of its way, rolling like a bright ball, scattering pins like a tiny porcupine shooting quills. Pick those up, said Catherine. Then I'll have my roses.

Morgantina drew an exquisitely wrought silver magnet from the pocket of her apron, and popped it under her tongue. Then she commenced to roll about the floor like a cat after mating. Pins leapt to her lips from everywhere; she seemed to devour them, uttering sounds of sharp delight. Catherine squealed with pleasure.

At last all the bright pins were gathered; the dwarf spat the tiny magnet delicately into her bodice; then she resumed her stitchery. Golden needle and thimble flashed back and forth, laden with heavy glass beads, false pearls, and precious moonstones, like drops of bright dew. Three more roses, Catherine prompted. In a glittering instant, there were three; a dazzling bouquet. The dress crumpled under its splendid burden. Catherine stood straighter, pulling at it, willing it to right itself. Now it is as ugly as you, she cried, plucking at the flowers. Stones flew; at last the silk gave way. Catherine tore at the stuff with her nails, shrieking. You've ruined it! I should have known better than to entrust you with such fine stuff. Now what will I do? Look at this! Not a shred can be saved. Answer me! What—

Vermilion! said Morgantina, in a bright voice. Vermilion was the queen's favorite color; it made her olive skin look yellow-green as one who had plague.

Vermilion? echoed Catherine, clapping her hands.

Morgantina's mouth set itself in an invisible line, like a careful seam. Not a trace of a smile.

THE PLAN HAS CHANGED, magician. Henry paced the shining squares outside Diane's studio. Cornelius waited, without reply. The lady Diane is still to be portrayed as goddess of the hunt, but only here, in this corridor and the salon. Elsewhere, as in the new chapel . . . The king's gaze wavered; his agitation was now palpable. Cornelius leaned forward, as though to comfort his patron, or to warn him of danger. Still he did not speak. Henry stepped backward in alarm. The Annunciation Scene, he said, quickening his speech. That great panel which the Jew who owned this house caused to be removed from the south wall.

If memory serves, said Cornelius softly. The removal was approved by the Church—

The king shrugged. That bishop, he said. That fool. Accepted a gift from the Jew. There were . . . disturbances. A fine was levied. It is of no consequence now. The time has come to replace the panel. A portrait of the Madonna—

The lady Diane, said Cornelius, with perfect understanding.

We want it so, said Henry. All in black. He gestured. But one breast.

Cornelius kept his expression blank. They will—they—

You will paint it, said Henry. Unless—

Cornelius bowed. The left breast, your Majesty?

Henry smiled. We shall leave . . . matters of composition . . . to the artist's judgment. The portrait must be ready in a month's time.

Cornelius, still bowing, made as though to withdraw, then paused. As to the angel, Majesty? he said.

Henry hesitated. As to the angel, he replied, meeting the painter's gaze for the first time. Then he shrugged. As to angels, we are indifferent.

IN A SECRET CHAMBER behind a door in the queen's private chapel, Morgantina sat at a low marble bench grinding her powders, distilling her liquid perfumes. Bottles stood about, and glass retorts, scales and measures, pestles and ewers, their contents glimmered darkly in the flickering candlelight: oils and essences to whiten the royal skin; potions to lighten the royal mood. It was said that Catherine sent to her native land for these rare ingredients; it was said that without them her face would be dark as a Moor's, and her humor blacker.

While she worked, the dwarf sipped a sweet liqueur from a tiny goblet made of exquisitely chased gold. This drink she prepared from crushed wings of butterflies, powdered shells of iridescent beetles, nectar of exotic flowers, and a certain flesh. Though she never spoke of it, many believed the elixir to be the potion on which her mother had weaned her, which stunted her limbs and gave her mysterious powers.

The tiny room was always fragrant with this liqueur, and with the essences in her beautiful jars—lime-colored heliotrope, myrtle like liquid sunshine, and, strongest of all, marescialla, an oil the color of burnished bronze, which bore the name of a beautiful marquise burned at the stake in the country of the Basques. It was said that as the marquise burned, the scent rose like a bronze cloud from her long white arms, coloring the air of the Pyrenées, lingering over the valleys like a fragrant lament. Years after her death, travelers swore they could tell if a man had passed through the village of Saint Pé, where she was buried; the odor of marescialla clung to his clothes and his body as though a perfumed arm had reached from the grave to caress him.

Yet though Morgantina often spent hours working in this cramped and airless room, she herself never carried the slightest trace of marescialla upon her clothes or her person. It was assumed that the liqueur banished all other elements with which she came in contact. At the same time it would shape her dreams. Often she would doze here, seated at her bench. Yet it was not a true sleep, not a restful slumber. It was the time, some said, when her limbs would extend to normal size, stretching long and shapely as the limbs of a marble goddess. She would feel the stone bench grow colder beneath her body, while her head grew lighter, softer than air. Soon unknown colors danced behind her eyes, in caverns of deep red, in opalescent darkness. Hours would pass, Morgantina knew not how many, but in the end she would behold her own fierce beauty etched in a glass stained with colors of fire. She would grow invisible, yet shining, an aerolith poised upon the crescent moon.

This night, after the reading of the magician, she worked with a feeling of unease. If Cornelius had discerned more than he would reveal, she must wrest it from him. A dwarf must possess her own secrets. Still, he could have feigned such a discovery—or imagined it. He would not be the first charlatan to be misled by his ambition.

But why then had a sudden searing pain struck her hand as she worked? For three days it had struck, every day at the same hour, even as she sipped the liqueur, even as her beauty danced in the splendid dark behind her eyes.

AN ARMY OF SKELETONS, covered each night with white robes, loomed in the moonlit dark of the corridor like a range of snow mountains. By day the robes were torn away, revealing ladders; painters scaled them to stroke the vaulted ceiling with colors of flesh and gilt, and the play of shadows. Robes billowed red and blue; swords flashed silver; black and spotted beasts reared and pounded great clouds of swirling dust. Below them a silent field of cloth lay spread upon the polished floor, catching bright rain from the painted heaven. In the stillness it seemed that at any moment the battle must overflow the walls, the drops would seep from true mortal wounds, scattering torn limbs and bloodstained armor. At a signal there must come the roar of pain, the clash of metal; words to these frightful stories; a great shriek of explanation. Chastity would tell how she came to be dressed for a wedding feast, running for her life in a streaming veil that tangled about her trembling limbs like pieces of pale ravaged sky. Lasciviousness would confess how he might pursue her, surrounded by a vicious pack of cripples and freaks, snarling, clawing, cloven-hoofed, the fur on their calves and torsos streaking like flames. They must all tell whose hell they were bound for.

Diane stood transfixed beneath the melee, her head thrown back, her lips parted. Is he not magnificent? she exclaimed, pointing to the monster. Is he not the very prince of air, the king of winds and dreams?

Henry made no reply. Instead he stood gazing out of the window, his back turned to the riotous work, and to Diane. I needed you this morning, he said, in a tone of accusation.

My dearest, she replied, did you forget how we planned this day? You were to send the couriers to me when you had done with them. You were to sign the notes. These workmen must be paid; I promised in your name—

Henry drew a sharp breath. Still his voice rose to an unmanly pitch. I warned you that this would happen; you would not heed. We cannot afford all this now. There is nothing with which to pay any of them, not a sou, not a florin, not a ducat, not a pearl.

Oh, said Diane, with a quick smile. Then I will put them off again. But you did promise to tell the ministers. Can they not call upon that banker, d'Estampes? Or the Jew. The one who wants d'Estampes' house? Have they considered the new tax you asked for? Have they done anything?

There is nothing, I tell you. Nothing can be done now. d'Estampes is bankrupt. There is no one left who can lend me a decent sum. For anything.

She studied him with a grave concentration. Then she whispered: Look, Henry, at my garden. How beautiful it is in this light. Shall we walk to the peach orchard? Or, no, to the stable. Cornelius' man has begun the modeling for the horse fountain. You remember?

Beautiful, he murmured. Gardeners must be paid too. And now Cornelius' man. And the stonecutter—

Diane shook her head. Do stop. We will let some of them go. They are a lazy lot. The gardeners lie about all

56

day, letting weeds choke the roses. As for the stonecutter, it is too bad. That great block of marble he sent does not ring true. It will have to be used for smaller works. She paused. Tell me how it went with Catherine.

He shrugged his shoulders but said nothing. She touched his hand, then withdrew, stiffened, drew herself in. He would not keep a secret from her long.

She—he began, and stopped. She—

Diane folded her arms and waited, gazing calmly at her roses with a distant smile.

Henry stole a look at her, then lowered his eyes. His face reddened. The dwarf, he said. She was there. I am certain of it. You know I cannot bear to be spied on at such a moment. Even by you. Even when we—

Ah, Diane murmured. My poor. My dearest. She paused. How do you know she was watching?

I felt it.

Perhaps you only dreamed it. One night you must forget these distractions. What matter if a creature lies between you? In fact or in fancy? So do I, after all. My body; my spirit; my love.

That is different, he said. You are *my* talisman.

She smiled. Come, she said. And tonight—

You are opening the salon? With this chaos in the hall?

It will be a further excitement, she said. I have invited only a small group, amusing chatterers. A simple meal. Two poets, or three, counting Strozzi. And that lovely singer, Anthea. We will play some games. Bring Catherine, if you like. Ask her if I can borrow her new forks.

I can't ask her that. You ask her.

Diane shook her head. I have not yet returned that book of sonnets I borrowed from her. She probably thinks I read them in bed. With you.

Don't you?

Certainly not. I merely lost the book.

Merely had the sonnets copied? Spilled wine on them? Gave them to that dark-eyed Italian lute player?

Are you teasing me, Henry? Don't tease me. I am far too upset. I am still in mourning, you know. And my poor head. I wake up in the night with such pain; today I thought I would go mad, worrying about these debts. I know I shall have to sell my poor jewels again. Even the diamond parure. Really, Henry, you must let me have charge of the crown jewels. You know I can pledge them more easily than you—and cause less gossip. And get a higher sum.

I don't know. I told you I would consider it. I don't know. Catherine would—

Diane sighed. Why must I always ask? I should not have to ask. If you loved me you would take better care of these matters.

You have the house—

A borrowed house. Diane smiled. Catherine could turn me out at a moment's notice—if she dared. While I pledge *my* jewels for the royal debts. To spare the royal embarrassment. *And* I have to plead with your servants, bribe them, to tend my beautiful things.

Diane, my beloved, don't vex me so. I will have the servants replaced.

It won't do any good; Catherine encourages everyone to be lazy or stupid when I need their services.

Nonsense; now it is you who are imagining devils.

Diane bit her lip. Henry, do let's go out. It is stifling here.

No, they are waiting for me. I told you. I have to appoint a new treasurer.

Not today. Oh, can't we let it all wait a day? How you

---

use these tiresome troubles to get out of enjoying things! Let your ministers take care of it. Come here. Let me— She tugged at his arm, pulling him into the studio. Let us—

Not here. Not now, he protested. Catherine will come to find me.

So? It will do her good. To see us. She stifled a conspirator's giggle. Henry, it will help you tonight. Here. And she dropped swiftly to her knees, pulling him down with her. Henry moaned softly as she unfastened him.

Ah, he sighed. And fit himself to her. All soft white rose cream. Ah.

A faint motion stirred the damask draperies, though there was no breeze. Morgantina the dwarf, nimble fingers flying, had begun to sketch what she saw, drawing their lover's knot, tying and untying as they did, with her soft brushes and her hard little heart.

Morgantina traveled through the palace by a system of tunnels, mouse and rat holes, cracks in walls, secret passages sealed and forgotten. Wherever whisperers gathered, or lovers or plotters, the dwarf conspired to be there. For whom did she spy? For Catherine, perhaps? Catherine thought so. Henry believed so. Diane, however, knew better. Morgantina spied for herself, as all outsiders must. There would come a day when a dwarf's ill-gotten secrets might serve an aging mistress. And so, even now, Diane's practiced eye followed the moving edge of the draperies, until it found what it sought—a barely perceptible flutter of the fringe, like the blink of a golden eyelash. Ah. Diane breathed in chorus with the king. Ahh.

When they had composed themselves and withdrawn, Morgantina remained at her post, motionless now as a dutiful sentry. It was her rule never to leave a room before it was empty, lest anyone discover her door and window, her corridor and passageway. Diane herself had sought them in vain, in every chamber, behind every curving stair. A dwarf covered her traces like the spoor of an animal.

HENRY AND CATHERINE have met by chance in the corridor; he is hastening toward Diane's house. The queen, sensing his discomfort at their encounter, seizes the moment. I have decided to take the magician with me, she announces, as though it is ordinary news. The man seems learned in matters of libraries, and the value of antiquities—

No. Henry frowns. It is not that he objects, but that he feels he must. Cornelius . . . has other duties here. The king gestures, vaguely, at the walls.

Catherine's face is smooth, her voice sure and light. She surprises herself. I know, she says. But I am certain he will earn his keep more surely if he accompanies me. You must know of the treasures he found for Cosimo, in Padua, buried in some dusty monastery. In any case, the new banquet hall must wait until my return. If I am still to be the model for Minerva? She smirks; it is not a pretty smile.

Henry glances at her sharply. He has a sudden thought. He brightens. This will do it. No. You have forgotten about the foreign princes who are coming to us. Without the magician, how shall we entertain them?

Catherine shrugs. I will leave you Morgantina. Why not let her perform her famous dance of love?

I hate freak shows. Henry shudders and makes a grimace. But he has become the petulant child, and Catherine seems untouched by his displeasure. She does not cast her eyes down; her shoulders fail to droop.

Do what you like, she says softly. But I shall take Cornelius. I am going for your sake. I am doing what you ask. But I shall have this. There is a peculiar authority in her voice.

Henry is startled into stuttering. His voice is thin and high to his own ear. All right, he says. But the rope of pearls. Do not fail—

HENRY IS SITTING in the courtyard like a punished child. He looks slyly about him, as though he knows someone has followed him, as though he must decide whether to greet that follower as a friend, or to leap up and strike him down like a thief. Perhaps both.

He has been squatting here for an hour, watching the Pan fountain playing water tunes upon a flute. He has been counting the tunes as he sits on the rough cobblestones. He does this often. He is sulking not so much over Catherine's decision to take Cornelius as over the assurance in her voice. Perhaps he only imagined this tone; still, it frightens him. She has grown larger, somehow; she looms. That is it; she looms. Henry cowers now, on the cobblestones. It is entirely unreasonable, he tells himself. She is the child; his consort, subject to him in all things. Subject to him. If he cannot control one small vicious female—but even now, thinking this, he feels himself beginning to sweat; he must stop this thinking. He reaches for the smooth black stone that hangs from a chain at his waist; he begins to stroke it. The coolness of it, the smoothness, calms him at once. Diane had given him this stone when he was a boy; it was, she said, a guard against certain poisons of the spirit. How fortunate he had been to meet Diane the year his mother died, in childbed, with his still-born sister. His mother. She who was called a vain beauty, a greedy tyrant; she who drove his father mad with her extravagance, her own madness, her wild ambition. Yet he remembered only how she would come to his bedside in the dark night, folding him in her white perfumed arms, singing to him. Songs of such sweetness they were, about the countryside of her childhood home, of enchanted woods and white-winged birds with jeweled beaks, of a boy destined to grow more golden than sunshine. Only Diane knew the words to those songs; Diane whose own white perfumed arms stirred memory or desire. He did not know how she had come to learn these words, born as she was in another land. Diane had not known Henry's mother; no one had ever spoken of her to Henry. He was raised by nurses and tutors, by footmen and sergeants-at-arms; Diane was lady-in-waiting to the new queen, his father's second wife. She was retired from service when the second queen died; by then Henry had come to love her. She was more than twice his age, yet her laughter was a shower of silver coins; she was a girl to him, more beautiful than the moon itself, that domain of her goddess namesake.

It was Diane who taught him to stand with his feet planted apart like strong young trees; she who instructed the royal tailors to pad the shoulders and the bodice of his doublet, to build a second Henry upon the first, a substantial Henry, a kingly Henry. She had the calves of his stockings discreetly padded; she had his thin neck disguised by a froth of lace like a cresting wave of the sea. Henry became a fine figure; his hats covered with plumes, his lank fine hair thickened with trimmings made from the fur of brave animals. The fashion of his country changed in homage to him; all men strove to cast a shadow like the king's.

Yet he would sit folded upon himself in the courtyard, fondling a stone for cold comfort. Frightened of a woman, a girl, a girl who was his, a girl who must bring him jewels to placate his creditors. What if she would not? What if she betrayed him to his enemies? Who now was not his enemy? The bankers ruined by their loans to the king? The king had promised to repay, had meant to repay. He needed things. He needed splendors. A king's needs were a king's right. A king's splendor was the kingdom's pride. Surely a banker understood; even if his own fine house must now be forfeit to pay his own creditors. Where now would Henry turn if Catherine brought no new fortune? If she failed him by design? A king must not think such thoughts. Diane, he thought instead. Diane must find a way to save him.

CATHERINE HAS SUMMONED Diane for an audience. She has never done this before. Still, Diane is entirely at ease, as always. It is infuriating.

So, she says to the queen, in a pleasant tone. It is said that you will take the magician. I wanted to give you this for the journey. Perhaps now you will not have need of it. She holds out a small casket of ruby-and-white swirled crystal, fastened with a golden clasp. Catherine opens it and gazes at the smooth dark stone within, gleaming like a jewel on blue velvet. Polished and perfectly round, it nestles in her palm; she closes her fingers over it.

It is just like Henry's, she says finally. He claims that it soothes him.

Diane smiles. It is a simple thing, but he believes that it serves him well in difficult times. I hope that its like will serve you.

Why? stammers Catherine. Why do you give me this?

Because, Diane replies smoothly, it is time for us to begin to be friends.

Catherine's face is hot. She thrusts the stone into its casket, flinging it from her. Friends! How can that be?

I can help you, says Diane. I do help you, even now. Do you not know that I do?

I cannot talk about these things. Not with you. I will not—you are—it is your fault that he—

No, says Diane, in a voice so gentle that Catherine feels it more than she hears it. It is a fault, but not of mine, your Majesty. Together we must overcome it, lest it bring down all—crown, country, Henry, Catherine.

The queen draws in her breath but is silent. She will not pronounce the name Diane. Even in a cold, mocking voice, she will not say that if Henry and Catherine fail to bear a child, it will bring down Diane as well.

You need my friendship, my Queen, Diane was saying. As I need yours.

Enemy, Catherine cried suddenly. Thief and whore. Traitor.

Yes, said Diane calmly. Some of those, surely; I do not deny it. But think. Thief of what is freely given, whore if one gives oneself in return. Enemy, traitor to whom? I am in your service, madam, and in your thrall no less than

64

your husband is in mine. We are entwined. She drew back the hem of her skirt; with a slender foot she traced the monogram etched in the white marble square she stood upon. It is a graceful design, she said.

Your design, said Catherine. Her tone was bitter. All of our lives; your cursed design. It is graven on my life.

And mine—

But you have no right, you have—

I have my destiny, madam. I have yours as well. I mean neither of us harm. We are as one . . . She reached out then, a white beautiful hand with its palm turned up, not to touch the queen, not in a gesture of beseeching, but only a hand offered, a hand so white, a slender hand that held a king; she held it out for Catherine now, as though there were another gift in it, an invisible treasure.

Catherine gazed at this phantasm; it seemed to glow. No, she whispered, not knowing what she meant to deny.

Why not? said Diane. Was it a taunt? It had the sound of a taunt.

Catherine had a sudden, bewildering impulse to touch that hand, or to flee, to stare at the hand until it vanished, to press the hand to her own breast. She turned swiftly to go, then, without thinking, bent to retrieve the black polished stone. The shattered casket of red-and-white crystal lay in bright shards upon the floor. She felt a fragment crunching under her heel; each step made a sound of breaking.

My queen, whispered Diane, dropping a curtsy, her voice as respectful as the curtsy itself. Yet Catherine heard a question, or a faint emphasis on the word "my," or a smile in the voice that might suggest something other than respect. She would not pause or turn her head. But the smooth dark stone, now clutched in her hand, felt slippery and warm.

∗   ∗   ∗

DIANE HAS ENTERED the dwarf quarters by means of the curved marble stairway from the queen's chapel. She crouches down to peer at the gold and ultramarine decorations on the walls, at the tarsia friezes, at the arms and devices, all in miniature size. A tiny scroll of music on azure ground, medallions and classical figures, globes and atlases, statuettes. An entire library of tiny books in Greek and Latin, mingled with romances of the day. An odd mix of museum, boudoir, doll house. Diane is both attracted and repelled, like all visitors here.

So this is the dwarf's lair, she says, not knowing what to say. It is quite . . . beautiful.

Morgantina looks at her sharply. It is a cruel joke, madam; you most of all must perceive it. Everything here is a toy, as I am. A reduction to absurdity.

But a splendid conceit. Diane runs her fingers appreciatively, knowledgeably, along the meticulously carved arm of a gilded chair. Everything is copied from Catherine's own treasures—the bed, the draperies. But these paintings, Diane says, are they copies too? I have never seen—

Morgantina grimaces to cover a surge of pride. These are mine; the queen does not permit me to hang them. When she is here they are stored away. Only the works of masters may grace these walls. An artist commissioned by their Majesties makes a miniature copy of his real work for my walls; it is agreed upon in his contract. She gestures. You will recognize—

Diane interrupts. And Cornelius? Is he represented here? Morgantina shakes her head as though to dispel the

66

notion. Not Cornelius, she murmurs. They begin to walk through the rooms, Diane nearly doubling over to edge through the narrow-arched doorways. She touches the carved basin of rock crystal, the tiny golden plates. She gazes awestruck at the damask hangings embroidered with legendary scenes: dwarf gods ravishing dwarf nymphs; each figure grotesque, misshapen, oddly beautiful. She pauses before a bronze statue of a naked hump-backed creature brandishing a bow.

Your namesake, madam, Morgantina says. Diana of the Hunt.

The tiny goddess stands with feet apart, defiant. Diane reaches toward it, then draws back her hand. I must go, she says suddenly. But the dwarf gestures toward the tea table; it is set for two, with a doll's set of dishes and pots made of rare porcelain. She seats herself and pours, proffering a tiny, exquisite cup. A gift, Morgantina murmurs, from one Eastern prince or another. Their Majesties' guests are kind to remember me always. Of course none of it belongs to me. It is Catherine's, all of it. I am, like you, most fortunate to serve here. It is not a bad life.

Diane nods. One grows accustomed—

Some grow, madam, says the dwarf. Others do not. She laughs; the sound is harsh.

Diane laughs too, but kindly. She is surprised that she no longer feels any discomfort. Morgantina's face alters; she wears, Diane realizes with a start, something like a genuine smile.

THE KING IS NOT USED TO being kept waiting in his mistress' rooms. She hurries to him now, flushed and merry, from her doll's tea party. But his face is a thundercloud. He almost snaps at her.

Well? Will it perform?

Diane takes his arm, making no reply for a moment. She will attend. We must invite her with respect. As a guest.

I won't have it near us. Catherine keeps her under the chair sometime, or behind her. He is still glowering.

Next to me, Diane says quietly. We'll seat her at her own table and chair, with her own dishes, all those beautiful little things. No one ever sees them unless they go to her rooms. And many shrink from—she smiles at her accidental jest—many like you, my Henry, do not appreciate the frisks of nature.

I do not like barbarisms. Nor trained animals at a feast. I would give all these creatures away—but Catherine will not part with them.

She smiles at him, moves closer to him, so that their bodies touch. Yes, she muses. I suspect she would be transformed from a sulking child to a madwoman.

He begins to melt; the warmth of her has penetrated all their clothing, touched his skin. Still, he says, it is time she grew up. Playing with that creature, shut up in that vault—that is probably what keeps her from quickening. She is stunted, like the dwarf.

Henry! She chides him softly, caressing him as she scolds. You know that is not—that is an excuse. We will cure this affliction together; but you must trust to it, as I do. Trust to us. She lifts her glass. The wine dances. She sips, then kisses him, letting the wine, warmed and flavored by her mouth, trickle gently into his. He takes it greedily, as a child, suckling. Ah.

———

∗   ∗   ∗

MORGANTINA STANDS UNCERTAINLY at the doorway of Diane's salon. You sent for me, madam.

Diane rises quickly from her writing table, as though to greet an honored guest. I wondered if you would care to walk in the garden? I want to ask your advice. It is said that you have the knowledge of flowers, the secret of the power in their essences.

Morgantina hesitates, watching Diane cross the room. The lady seems agitated; she is taking care not to move too close. Both her gaze and her words float toward the window, out into the air, as though she would fling them anywhere but to Morgantina. I have some knowledge, madam, replies the dwarf, keeping her voice so soft that Diane must turn to catch it, must finally turn to meet her eyes. Shall we walk together, then?

They walked in a way Morgantina never walked with Catherine, the lady Diane slowing her step so that the dwarf need not race to keep up, need not roll and hobble breathless as a small dog nipping at the queen's heels. Diane turned often, as though to take her measure. She would draw the dwarf out with strange questions, more appropriate to a lady of rank. How had Morgantina come to be as she was? Yet it was not a challenge; she did not tease Morgantina in the way of sport, as the queen's visitors often did: Have you wit? do you dance? are you chaste? were you born thus, or made? Rather, Diane spoke like a young girl prodding a distant cousin or a visiting princess, chattering in a royal nursery. What do you think of this or that? The sun on the roses, the poet's lament for

69

his lost love (and who was she?), the cook's new gooseberry tart. Twice Morgantina found herself laughing like an innocent; she recovered her gravity with a start. Delight is not a proper game for a dwarf.

Shall I tell you a secret about myself, Diane said suddenly, her wide gray eyes round as a child's. No—I shall tell you three, and one will be false. You must guess which. Morgantina nodded warily, her whole body tense with distrust. Once, said Diane, in a conspirator's tone, once I loved a woman. Morgantina made no reply. Another time, Diane went on, I loved a child of ten. Still Morgantina was silent. And once, Diane said at last, now leaning to whisper into Morgantina's ear, I loved a monster.

That is an easy mystery, my lady, said the dwarf. The last is a lie.

And not the other two? Diane asked, laughing.

The others are lies as well, said the dwarf. For all three loves are the lady Diane, and she loves not herself.

Oh, said Diane softly. You are not so wise after all. For you would not speak so to one who could do you harm.

Morgantina smiled. Anyone can do me harm, madam. That is what I am for. You, however, have another interest in me.

And what do you imagine that is?

Morgantina must choose her answer with care. You are interested in my likeness to you. Your beauty is my ugliness, your wit my folly—

Diane colored, again feeling ill at ease. She stopped walking and stood facing the dwarf, breathing as though it were she who must run to keep up. Morgantina seemed to take no notice but strode on past Diane, then slowly turned. Favorites are in all ways alike, she said, in a tone of kindness. A dwarf cannot be kind, of course; when a dwarf speaks kindly, the words have a sound of arrogance. A dwarf has no equals; no one who must bend and reach down to stroke one's hair can be a friend. Favorites, she said, are those who may soon be out of favor. Riddle me this, my lady: when is a favorite ill-favored?

When she falls from favor, Diane replied, without hesitation. For then she is nothing. Is no one.

Now the dwarf would change the subject. What advice did you seek? These roses will not last the summer. She knelt to touch a ravaged leaf. They are under attack.

What must be done to save them?

You must sacrifice some, said the dwarf, or you will lose all.

Tell me what to do.

I cannot. You must cut them down, or pull them up and replace the soil. Else the queen's garden will be ravaged as well.

Diane said nothing. The dwarf shrugged her good shoulder. This rose is very beautiful still. Viewed from your blue salon there will seem nothing amiss here. And in a certain light—it will be some time before—

Diane sighed. Will you come tonight?

And perform for the king's guests? With the queen abroad?

I said nothing about performing.

But I have understood perfectly what you have not said.

Diane frowned. Are we never to trust each other in anything? She reached out suddenly and laid her hand, fingers curled outward, against the dwarf's cheek. The dwarf leaned her head against the coolness. Never, she said. Never is best.

THE QUEEN, WITH HER MAGICIAN and her retinue, has been kept waiting many days in the papal palace. Their rooms are splendid; servants spring to attend their slightest wish; Cornelius is free to search the countryside for treasures. Each day the Pope, Catherine's cousin, promises to receive her the next. And each day sends word of some new reason for delay. Cornelius attends the queen constantly, calming her with mysterious remedies.

At last the audience is granted. In the final hour before the meeting, Catherine sends for the magician. He prepares a calming potion. She drains the phial, sinks wearily upon her cushions, closes her eyes. He stands over her, moving his hands, enclosing her in a casket of air. Are you afraid? he whispers. Do you believe the Pope will refuse you what you ask?

On the contrary, she replies, in a dreamer's voice. I expect he will grant all my requests. And exact a terrible payment.

Cornelius moves about the bed, making his silent, priestly gestures, touching her. Does he not trust that you will repay his generosity? Is he not compassionate, your kinsman? Have you come to ask more than what he is pledged to give you—more than is yours by right?

Catherine sighs, frowning, still with her eyes closed. How little you pretend to know of the world, my worldly friend! My cousin rose to the papal throne by all the means usual to his profession. The trading of favors, of pledges for favors. Did you not know—payments are always highest when the need for favor is greatest? One promises what one must; one pays when one can. And if the payment is late, the penalties rise.

Cornelius pauses in his movement, like a dancer awaiting his music. But you are not yet in his debt?

Catherine breathes another sigh. We have so far been fortunate. But he would rid us . . . of witches and magicians. He would have us more vigorous in our piety. He suspects me—he knows my beliefs. My weaknesses.

Cornelius smiles, continues his circling, his touching and not touching. He will demand more burnings, then. More driving out of imaginary demons. It is easily done.

Catherine nods. A good riddance. My cousin is zealous in God's work. It is his monument. With the stake, the rack, and the righteous sword, he wins much treasure for the Church. He wonders why Henry's court remains infamous, why those who flee from the true way find safety with us. Why we permit witches and sorcerers to hide in our mountains. Why we keep them safe in our seaside villages. He believes we have become friends with the devil. Our soldiers fail to do God's work; is it because our treasury is low—or because we are lax in our own souls?

Now Cornelius stands silent behind the queen, his hands resting upon her brow. Majesty, he whispers. Promise him a thousand infidels. Pledge him the fierce light of your faith. He will pay his promised gems; there are quick ways to keep the bargain.

Catherine's eyes fly open. Oh, Cornelius, she says. Do you not think we have lost good men and gold in those mountains, chasing those evil phantoms? The Pope believes there are tens of thousands hiding with stolen gold, performing their obscene rituals in perfect safety. He believes—no, he knows with a certainty—that they unearth the bodies of children from their innocent graves, that

---

73

they cut down hanged men to draw their blood, that there are werewolves again in Saint Pé, and wild dancing women shaking their hair to draw down the moon. I would swear he had gone mad, but everyone believes him. Even in the cities. His inquisitors, his soldiers, all swear they have seen, they have heard, they know all these stories are true.

Cornelius is silent for a moment. Gently he presses the queen's eyelids closed. Then he says, Madam, you must believe his truth. You must offer your royal hand upon his holy bargain.

Catherine replies softly, drowsily, Speak with care, magician.

Cornelius smiles to himself, with his eyes solemn. Well I know the danger, madam; I have lived this life before.

DIANE HAS SENT WORD to the king: Morgantina will dine with us tonight, after all. The poor creature is turning into a mushroom down there, in that dank chamber of tiny horrors.

Henry finds his lady in her garden. They walk together. Henry says: I thought you found the dwarf as loathsome as I do.

Diane smiles without replying to this. It seems inhuman to keep her imprisoned all these weeks. Anyway, the Countess de G—— is coming, she adores freaks. Besides, we haven't any other entertainment. That singer you liked refused to perform again unless we pay him.

Scoundrels and ingrates, says Henry, without feeling.

Diane shakes her head in agreement. No respect anymore for the royal summons. Can you believe what is happening to musicians? Not to speak of artists.

Henry sighs. Morgantina has grown fat, lazy, and stupid in the queen's absence. Though she will have to do. They turn back toward the palace.

Diane plucks a white rose, fastens it to the king's coat. The feast will be splendid, she says. I am sure of it.

Henry is mollified. A dwarf can be amusing between two wines, he says. Diane kisses him for his wisdom.

MORGANTINA SLIDES TO THE FLOOR from her tiny chair; a comic pratfall. Ford the river! cries a nobleman. The dwarf gazes at him, her wide eyes unblinking. Ford the river! he shouts again. Morgantina rises to her feet and flings her skirts high over her head, turning slowly like a lewd mechanical toy upon a music box, the candlelight throwing shadows like spears upon her naked limbs. Sudden laughter rings through the great feasting hall like a rush of angry water. Morgantina turns and turns until the laughter dies; then she lets go her fistfuls of whirling silk and lace; the skirts descend around her with a sigh; she bows her head; she curtsies; she sinks upon her velvet tasseled cushion. A hail of sweetmeats, chestnuts, sugar drops follow her descent. She gathers them in her lap, bows her head, doubles over, and remains still for an instant. Then she bobs up again with a great round cake held in her teeth, a cake almost as large as her face. Delighted roars now fill the hall; footmen spring forward to refill wine goblets, to bring new platters piled high with roasted peacocks wearing all their feathers. Morgantina has been a success; no one will notice the wine is watered, the birds cleverly sliced so thin that painted roses on the plates could be seen through them but for the gravy. All would agree that the lady Diane has never looked more enchanting. What are those faint lines about her eyes? Surely not worry or care? Well, how old can the woman be? Fifty, sixty? And there is Henry bravely carrying such heavy burdens of state upon his scrawny shoulders. The padding of his splendid new coat transforms him utterly. How fares the little queen on her journey? One hears she is already laden with priceless treasures, unearthed from heaps of monkish dust. Paintings and antiquities, rare books from the Pope's own library. It is said she will return wearing the famous rope of pearls. Henry's credit will be restored. There will soon be enough gold for an expedition. For an army. Horses and armor. Ships and victories. If only the little foreigner were not barren, what a fine queen she would be.

Morgantina lowers herself now, spread-eagle upon a square of silk-embroidered carpet; the musicians strike up a melody, notes rapid as strokes of a sword or the thrusting of a violent lover. As they beat upon their instruments, faster and faster yet, her body echoes them, beating itself against the carpet as though she were being hurled or flung. Her head twists like a puppet's; her hair bounces and flies about her huge head as though pulled by a vicious wind. She bobs like a cork upon water, writhing, shaking under the blows of unseen fists or clubs. Now she turns a somersault, now lies prone, shaking as before, striking the carpet again and again. Courtiers and guests smile; trays pass from one to another. A lady plucks a sugar drop from a stem, another pops one into the open mouth of the nobleman at her side. I do not like these freak acts, he whispers.

Nor do I, she replies. But they are all the rage in Italy. One hears of nothing else. Barbaric, says another. Look at that creature; she mocks the art of love with her grotesque mime.

The grotesque thing is that her body makes human motions of any kind. Such creatures are made to be still, so that one may study their perversity.

I prefer statues of them to the real thing; you need not look at their eyes. The ancients made them seem almost lovable. Like monkeys.

Still, look at her! She is a marvel; the gestures are exactly those of a maid being ravished by lions.

Have you ever seen a maid ravished? By a lion?

Madam, I was the lion. (Laughter.)

Can you imagine those motions on a bed? I mean if the body were one whit less repulsive—

How do you think your body would look doing such a trick?

My last lady assured me I looked like Apollo riding his chariot.

And what became of that lady?

Alas, she renounced me for a mortal. (Laughter.)

AT THE PAPAL PALACE, Cornelius has burst into the queen's bedchamber, unannounced. He is in a fever of excitement. Look at the prize I have found for you, Catherine. He holds up a rare book on which he has been laboring. The fine pages are transparent, luminous. Catherine wears a look of boredom, of annoyance. Another old book, she snaps. Have we not enough of those by now?

Look, madam, says Cornelius, proffering his treasure. This one is not what it seems. Monks have been at it, but wonders lie beneath their pious work. He holds a single page to the light. With painstaking care, he has erased the psalms, the prayers and meditations copied in a spidery hand. From beneath spring forth poems of profane love; words like dancers in a wild formation, like rings of exotic flowers. My little queen, Cornelius says, his voice soft as in prayer. We shall make your husband's fortune with this treasure. And your own fame, queen of all art and refinement.

Catherine shrugs. I have yet to achieve my mission here. Henry's emissaries grow weary. Those rogues who went to Naples and the East in search of other treasure brought back nothing, not enough to repay the cost of their own journey, let alone mine. Thieves. I know they pocket the best of what they purchase; we have never yet profited from such ventures.

Majesty, muses Cornelius, sifting through her caskets of jewels. Will you carry the pearls on your person for the long journey home? There are many who know of their worth, many who might fetch a fortune merely for breaking the rope. A single pearl can be sold to any stranger, without risk. Unlike the fine work of your goldsmiths, these gems are unmarked, therefore unprotected. You must consider another way to carry them.

Catherine eyes him sharply. I have already thought of it.

How, may one ask?

Look at these linens, these fine embroideries, this lace. So many craftsmen, my countrymen, have sent gifts. They wish only to hear their praises sung; to have their goods admired by noblemen in a distant land. To say that Catherine poured her salt from their cellar. That she ate the tight green flowers from their wild seeds, and thus conceived a child.

Everyone wants only to be immortal, madam.

Yes, well. I have asked for one other thing, a spread for my bed. That bed with the great posts of turned gold furling upward like the curls of angels. I want a spread for it, the color of twilight, sewn with pearls like scattered stars. A perfect replica of the heavens. A spread brilliant as a sky. False pearls, of course. It is a conceit. When I lie upon it, I shall be queen of heaven. I have engaged twenty seamstresses to copy the finished spread when it arrives. I will break the rope myself, to provide the false pearls for the second one. No one but I shall know which spread carries the treasure.

Cornelius' eyes fill with something like rapture. What a cunning queen this unpleasant child would someday make.

THE LADY DIANE encounters the dwarf outside her salon. The visit is unexpected, but Diane shows no sign of surprise. She nods graciously. Morgantina offers no explanation. May one mention the new portraits, my lady? she asks, in a light voice. It is said you are dissatisfied.

Who says it? No matter; it is true. Cornelius is a dauber like the last one. Indifferent.

Perhaps his hand needs warming, says Morgantina. I have seen his work; he has an eye for detail.

Diane sniffs. But none for the big picture. We want monuments here. We have enough miniatures. No offense.

Morgantina nods her great head. None taken. But if I may suggest, he needs a serious project—not another Hercules; no more Seasons; enough of Chastity and the Vices. A monument requires a monumental idea.

79

I have run out of those. Diane sighs.

I have been thinking, my lady. Morgantina begins to speak rapidly; she skips about the corridor, gesturing. What we could use is a really major edifice. I mean something to uplift the eyes and hearts of people in this dark time.

Diane listens intently. She knows well how empty the royal coffers are. We could unveil it, says Morgantina, rushing on, when the foreigners come at the next great feast day. Not a mere fireworks, or rare prancing animals. A thing that will remain forever. Years from now, it will stand, bearing witness. The world will come to gape, whispering with awe the names of Henry and Catherine. And Diane, of course. She stops abruptly, cocking her head.

Diane has grown thoughtful. Something that echoes Henry through the ages. But what must it be? A tower? The world's tallest obelisk? Men like obelisks.

Something more personal. Morgantina smiles.

I was imagining a statue of Henry, Diane muses. For that fine empty space at the center of the garden maze. High up on a great pedestal, a colossal piece hewn from a single block of stone. Some fragment of a Roman temple. Something Visigothic—

And the king galloping? His fine charger rearing; his rein firmly held.

Diane bursts into sudden laughter. And his finger in his mouth. Have you seen the king ride? At breakneck speed? Charging swift as a mad centaur, with his finger in his mouth! He bites and sucks with all the fury of a child weaned too soon.

A child, says Morgantina softly, who flees for his life, with death at his heels.

Diane's expression changes; there is a bitter edge to her reply. For his life, or against. I know not. Though of all people, I have reason to know.

You *are* his very life, madam, says the dwarf. He draws breath from you, and fire, and courage.

Catherine is his life, Diane says harshly. His court is his life. I am merely his amusement. A muse, as you know, may be a fool.

Never less so than in your case, my lady. This king is a black swan who mates forever in his animal heart.

Diane smiles coldly. Would such a swan give me the crown jewels for safekeeping, do you imagine? Pledges must be made on the diamond parure, the ruby sword, the crown itself, if the new works are to begin. Artisans must buy their stones—

Artisans have bought on promises before—even on imagined promises.

And those whose work is not completed, or does not satisfy, have died in debt. Leaving widows and children to dine on the promises.

I know, madam. My father was such. It was I who saved the family in the worst time. Fortune smiles often upon the caprices of her own nature.

Diane stares at the dwarf, as though at a stranger.

What happened to your mother? she asks, gently.

Morgantina's tone is ice. My mother made the cage in which I shrank from growing. It was said that she knew, at the moment of each birth, which of her children would become great, which small. And which would be both. So you see me, as my mother fashioned me. With Fortune's blessing.

My mother knew me not, Diane whispers. Nor did Fortune. We are both become our own creatures.

With respect, madam, says the dwarf, I am not my own creature.

Diane reaches forth her hand, not quite touching Morgantina. With equal respect, my poor friend, she says, neither am I.

THE QUEEN HAS RETURNED from her journey, laden with diverse treasures. The king is well served; still, he withholds his praise. A king does not stoop to praise his wife, lest she mistake it for her due. Catherine withdraws into her blackest mood, nursing her bitterness; she is more than ever a stranger in this court.

The dwarf is summoned. Catherine wishes to torment something other than herself. Did you miss me? she demands, eager to begin the vicious game. I hear you danced for Diane. I hear she had all your little treasures moved upstairs for the feast. And the gentlemen found you dreadful.

Morgantina curtsies. All praise was for her Majesty's exquisite taste in all things. Great care was taken to display her favorite objects, to recount the brilliance of her choices, the vastness of her knowledge, her discerning eye. All agreed. No eye, no appetite for beauty matches Catherine's. Even the famed scholars praised her. Even the learned curators. Of course Strozzi read the most rapturous new sonnet about her, along with the old ones he had dedicated to her. And the king amazed all with his praise of his adored wife. The lady Diane glowered when he spoke, yet on he prattled, heedless of her dismay.

Liar, said Catherine, pinching her here and there. But the queen's cheeks glowed; her pinches were halfhearted.

Morgantina bore them bravely; her mistress' dull eyes seemed almost bright.

The dwarf smiled. And there were excellent reports of your journey, Majesty. It was said your words made the Pope's heart melt into a river of gold.

Hardly a river. Scarcely a rivulet. My kinsman has the heart of a bargainer in an Oriental bazaar. I had to pledge terrible things.

Your first-born child? Morgantina's eyes narrowed. Not that, said Catherine; she seized the dwarf's nose, gave it three sharp twists, as though it were the knob of a secret door that must spring open. Instead it came off in her hand. Catherine held it aloft and smiled. I promised him the nose of Morgantina, she said. For a start.

After the dwarf repairs her damaged face, the two lie far apart, at opposite ends of the queen's great bed. They have shared a healing draught and are waiting for their dreams to begin. Musicians in the courtyard below play a gentle, insistent air, repeating and repeating like a flowing stream. The dwarf is in her famous sleeping posture: legs crossed, toes tucked in her ears, head resting on her feet as on a cushion. She lies at the foot of the bed, as distant from the queen as possible. Catherine lies stretched out at the edge of the bed nearest to the window, so that she can hear the musicians' fingers touching their strings. Her ear is exquisitely tuned, thanks to the potion. She can imagine the flute player's breath in her ear.

How does your Majesty now? Morgantina whispers.

I am cold, I am sick, you have poisoned me.

It will pass, Morgantina says. It is but a moment before the moment.

O, you are a liar as well as a poisoner. You have killed me.

Morgantina stifles a laugh. Your Majesty well knows

it is always like this, just before the moment. Only hear the music, like a fall of water; let it strike the smooth stones and begin its descent. Soon you will enter the red dream. Breathe against the music, Majesty.

Catherine drew a breath, and another. It is no use, it is no better, you have tricked me again, monster! But suddenly her voice softened. Wait, she said, it is beginning. The light quivers, there, do you see it?

Ah, said Morgantina. Tell me.

I cannot. It is dark now. Too dark.

Light the taper.

Yes. I see. Velvet walls. And the witches' dream.

Are you alone?

The queen starts. What are they doing here? Look, Cornelius is whispering to her, his lips are twisted, they will do me a harm, he will teach her—

Ahhh. Morgantina's voice grew gentler. Hmmm. It was a song without words, a vibration of breath, cool fingertips of pure sound. Ahhmmm.

Catherine's breath quickened. She squirmed upon the bed, as though a strong hand had seized and shaken her. Then she subsided, limp as a wind-tossed flower. Water, she whispered.

Majesty? The dwarf brought water; Catherine raised herself to drink.

What are you staring at, creature? The queen's voice was restored. What has happened? It is black as night.

Time has passed without traces, Morgantina said. Do you not feel refreshed?

I feel—as one waking from sleep. Yet I have not slept.

You must use this tonight, said the dwarf, proffering a small container of salve. The body must be anointed.

84

Rub it well upon the lower part of the trunk; then pour one drop into each of the seven openings to the temple of the body.

The queen lowered her gaze. I am to have myself embalmed with your vile fluids? She sniffed. It smells horrid. What's in it? She wrinkled her nose with distaste. A certain flesh—I have heard of its evil origin. Some babe still warm in its grave—

All natural ingredients. Liquid essences. No harmful substances. Nothing to cause rash or fever.

Nothing to cause disturbing dreams? Nothing to damn the unwary soul?

I cannot know which dreams disturb your Majesty's rest, and which enhance it. As to the soul—

You do know. You mix the proportions. You control it. It was you who made me see devils and fire that first time. And the other time, you caused me to imagine handsome youths, feasting, beautiful gardens.

And which did you prefer?

I hated them all. Cursed witches' visions! I know well the tales of your ancestresses. Did they not charm the very judge who burned them? He had only to see them pass, lifting their bright hair to the breeze, letting the sun kindle it. Small wonder that he made them dance into their own fire.

Morgantina makes no reply to this. Instead she says: The king will lie with you tonight.

And the devil have the fruits.

How does your Majesty know that curse?

From those same witch trials at Saint Pé. From those women who would sooner spend themselves in lust with the devil than bear a child.

They feared not the bearing of children, Majesty. Only

the bearing of children who must starve at the breast. May the devil have the fruits! So I heard my mother pray.

How fortunate for her to have the prayer answered. The devil gave her Morgantina!

The dwarf unfolds herself, rises from the bed, curtsies. Fortunate for us both, Majesty.

HENRY HAS SENT FOR the magician. A matter of some urgency. We need new tricks, he says; beneath his coat, his fingers fidget, stroking a smooth black stone. He looks sidewise at Cornelius, wondering if the man can tell. New tricks, he says again, louder. Our creditors have discovered too many of the old ones.

Cornelius ponders. Perhaps a new feast day? Why not celebrate something? The queen's return—or the Pope's promises? Guests never see what you are after, if you fill their goblets and their eyes.

Henry sighs. Puffs of colored smoke won't do it this time. We need ships and armor. We need those fortifications. We need other men's fortunes to repair our own.

The magician nods gravely. Still, he says, a feast day always impresses the foreigners. I can do a lot with the leftovers. And all I will need this time is—whatever the royal coffers have set aside for such occasions.

The king's smile is twisted; he thrusts out his empty hand and turns it in an elaborate gesture. Do you not understand, magician? The royal coffers contain nothing that you yourself cannot conjure. That is the reason for this show. Promise your paint merchants, your silk traders, your jugglers, your workmen, promise whomsoever you will, whatsoever you must. All will be richly paid when the success of this show is assured. And only then.

Cornelius pales. But how—?

The king shakes his head, holding up the same empty hand in a gesture of warning. How should the king know how the magician works his magic? If the king knows, it is no magic.

Cornelius bows and withdraws. He would pack his poor belongings and leave at once. He must find another court, another master, one with fewer debts; one with fatter, idler servants, dressed in silks and blessed with the leisure to write poems. He should have foretold that this day would come. The beguiler is always beguiled.

THAT NIGHT CORNELIUS nibbled the last of his sugar dwarf humps and was rewarded with a fortunate dream. The dwarf was there, scurrying across the gallery over the green river, from the palace and its spreading wings to the white house of the lady Diane. In the dream that house seemed to tremble as though it were a temple of spun sugar upon a festal cake. The dwarf floated silently across the marble squares in her soft little shoes, carrying a message from the queen to her rival. It was an invitation; the lady Diane must come this night to dine with the queen; there would be an entertainment, amusing new guests, a great poet and dramatist, scandalous bawdy minstrel songs, lewd dances, terrific magics. There would be a hunt for hidden treasure, a game of chance, a hide-and-seek in the garden maze, a masque. Each guest must come dressed as a god, a nymph, a satyr, a tyrant of history.

But all must end the evening disguised as the dwarf, naked, misshapen, festooned with magnificent pearls.

Cornelius awoke knowing what he must do. He must sell what he could steal of the queen's new treasure. That rare book of ancient love poems? A few paintings. A handful of pearls from the fabled rope. And the miniature figure of an ancient dwarf, an exquisite enameled object of fantasy, its tongue, hands, and head so delicately balanced as to be set in motion at the slightest touch, at the wave of a hand or the breath of a tender breeze. Any of these things might fetch a price that would at least persuade a supplier of orange smoke or sticks of fire. And one artisan in turn would tell another that the king's coffers were full, full enough to pay for a week of revels. The magician smiled. Tomorrow he would begin to conjure a king's ransom out of thin air.

THE QUEEN IS SEATED at her looking-glass, glowering. The magician enters, looking agitated.

The king insists that I wear the pearls, Catherine says. We must have the rope restrung. Bring me the brooch that bears my ancestress' likeness. There is no other image of the rope's design. Not even a drawing.

Cornelius says lightly, What matter if it differs in some detail? If it be three inches shorter, or has five strands entwined, instead of six?

Catherine turns to glare at him. What matter? Shrewd eyes will be fastened to it. The rope is fabled—poets have written of it. Six strands there are, each of a thousand pearls of breathtaking size, braided thick as a sailor's rope;

then bound, and at the ends, a cascade of twenty-five single pearls, larger and more lustrous than the rest, hanging loose down to here. The whole must be thick enough to twine about the body three times, like the rope that binds a prisoner; it is a fine conceit. The thing must weigh so heavily that when it lies coiled upon a cushion, two pages struggle to bear it.

Cornelius tries another tack. He wants you bound so, through the entire evening? You will scarcely support such a monstrosity. You will faint.

Catherine is not swayed. Henry says we must show them everything we've got. The jeweled collar and the headdress, and that awful ruby-studded belt that the old queen gave me. My mother's amber rosary with the tortured saints. All the ugly pendants— She sighs. How are things going with the entertainment?

Cornelius hesitates. Shall he tell her he plans a Dionysian revel? Is the mood of the court right for a scandal? Do they want something modern or classical? Can they bear bawdiness spiced with a mild heresy? Will the foreigners adore it, or find it obscene? All goes well, madam, he says, and leaves it at that.

THOUGH HE SAT IN THE POSE of wisdom and clarity, with his legs folded and his eyes softly closed, though he inhaled the slow breath of tranquillity and exhaled the slower one of concentration, though he held in his left hand the powerful globe of polished amethyst, and in his right the smaller, sympathetic one of pure crystal, still Cornelius felt the old fear rising in him, the old knowledge that this time, even bold action might not save him. The king would have his pagan revel; the Pope would take his hostages; the queen would make her sacrifices; the lady Diane would make her show of strength. But would the magician make his escape?

There was nothing to be done but the thing itself: the revel, the sacrifice. It would be as in the ancient time, a logical following of death upon the heels of violent life. If only he could foretell the sacrifice. He had tried the mirror, and the crystal, and the three vases. He had cast the drop of oil into the vial of water. And his own geometric system, an intricate pattern of dots, randomly cast and recast. All these yielded nothing but the old images: beardless youth, prison, constraint. He had sold all but a few of the stolen pearls from the queen's rope; the largest one he shut up in an earthen pot to enchant it. One by one he uttered the names: Morgantina, Diane, Henry, Catherine—and Cornelius. Yet the pearl would not leap, would not strike against the pot, would not yield up its enchanted knowledge. Perhaps the pearl was false. Perhaps it was one that would yield only the name of a thief, not an innocent. He must attend to the planning of revels, yet the chill of his fear would not subside. He must rouse himself.

CATHERINE RUMMAGED AMONG her treasures, seeking that strange painting which Cornelius had persuaded her to buy, despite the certain knowledge that her cousin the Pope had twice ordered it destroyed. What a piece of mystery it was, with its three parts joined like a holy work, yet crowded with blasphemies, whose meaning must be clear only to a madman. Had its perverse beauty delivered it each time from the holy flames? Or was it the devil's own hand that saved it? In part to ease her conscience, she had paid the thief who brought it to her with false pearls. It was said that he had cut open his thigh to smuggle them across the high mountains to his band of strange fugitives. Brothers of the Free Spirit, driven from village to village, followed by tales of their evil powers. Still, they huddled somewhere, eking out their poor lives, clinging to their orgiastic ceremonies, burrowing in caves, hiding their evil from God's eyes. Catherine could not take her own eyes from the painting; it had invaded her dreams, waking and sleeping. Here was a monster with blasted trees for limbs, mired in a muddy stream. His body a broken wooden vessel, leaking noxious fluids; his human face gazing backward with a look of sorrow. And here was a creature whose body was a pair of monstrous ears, scuttering on the legs of an insect. Naked corpses with human forms and heads of animals lay about in obscene postures; figures in priests' robes ate of each other's flesh or fornicated with their own severed parts.

Cornelius had said it was a master's work, that it celebrated the innocent birth of human life, even of its evils, even of carnal love, for all of these were the work of God. One panel glowed like hellfire, another shone dark as earth, or excrement; the third shimmered in all the colors of water or air, and was peopled with ghostly seraphic creatures that flew or swam, though they had neither limbs nor wings nor fishes' tails, and their transparent bodies were the same changing colors as the opaline substance through which they traveled.

Catherine sat before the painting in a half dream, entering each of the painted realms of light and darkness, each of the bodies of the damned and the angelic. Was this the work's holy purpose? Was it an altarpiece to inspire the faithful, who celebrated their own bodies, made in God's image? Rapture and awe, pleasure and terror. Catherine knew such prayer was blasphemy. Yet she gazed and dreamed, and felt a strange heat in her body, as though a fever stirred it.

What if Henry's pagan revel were modeled upon this painting? A pageant both splendid and mad, its meaning and origin mysterious, unlike the Hellenic orgies savored by some princes who had lived to regret them. It was true that women would rather cloak themselves in transparent veils than portray monsters. Diane would much prefer to come as Nero's wife, wrapped in invisible silk—fold upon fold of sheer shining stuff that concealed none of her secrets but her ambition. Which lady would dare come as a pair of ears, or a severed tongue? Well, they could take liberties in the dressing of their hair. An Eve without jewels; an Adam without gold. Creatures of fantasy could wear hide and hair, tusks and cloven hooves, two heads or three. Cornelius must have a great cavern dug in the palace ground, above it a splendid garden, a crystal fountain of life, naked children swimming about in it. And within the cavern itself, darkness still and soft as a great womb. Creatures tumbling in and out, deer and great birds grazing above, trees hung with strange flowers and unknown fruit, while underfoot coiled iridescent serpents and toads bearing their jeweled warnings.

I don't know, said Henry, when Cornelius described the queen's plan. It all sounds a little dark. I had something gayer in mind. He turned to Diane. What do you think?

Diane had listened well, sifting her calculations. Such a pageant would be a horror, a spectacular scandal. The bishops would blame Cornelius, brand him atheist, libertine. She was not yet ready to have him ruined. Or, rather, she preferred to design his ruin herself. She sighed. Oh, not another Garden of Eden. Everyone has done it. One must begin a feast wearing magnificent robes, and then remove them as the mood grows merrier. Not the other way around. I fear our Cornelius does not understand the way of celebrations.

Henry agreed; a vigorous nod, with a forceful kingly frown. Diane scarcely paused to wait for it. A simple festival of the grape, she said. Everything white and green. Games in the maze. Nymphs, fauns—satyrs, if you insist. Lutes and flutes. The usual. One must do it simply, as the ancients did. We have many drawings. Cornelius himself has brought them to us.

Yes. Henry clapped his hands. Yes. And what about the puffs of orange fire? The clouds, the singing Vices? All that . . . as you said you had done for the Italians?

Cornelius bowed. All that . . . as you wish.

Perhaps, said Diane, if all goes well, we can do the Millennium next time.

ALL DID NOT GO WELL. At first Cornelius thought the dwarf was to blame. It must have been she who persuaded the queen to set costly new wine tasters upon every table, sumptuous golden bowls engraved with adders' tongues, sharks' teeth, fragments of narwhal posing as unicorn horn. Cornelius had warned the king against such foolish measures, such an ostentatious display of fear. Rumors of poison preceded every feast day of late; cautionary tastings were properly done in the kitchens, in the wine cellars, not at the table before one's honored guests—especially not before guests from whom one hoped to extract both gold and conspicuous friendship. But the king was not persuaded.

To make matters worse, the dwarf fell into a deathly faint beneath the queen's table, setting off a panic that neither wine nor music could drown. In the confusion, some thief had pilfered the most beautiful of the tasting bowls, one studded with precious stones, enameled with lively color, ringed round with fluted gold and with crystal set in the new way, so that it gave a sparkling imitation of diamonds. A coincidence, perhaps, that it was graven all about with powerful symbols against harm: sun and moon, pelican, phoenix, and laurel tree. It was possible that the thief was also the poisoner; possible that Morgantina had been an unintended victim; she had scarcely sipped her thimbleful of the magnificent wine. I am poisoned, I am dying, she thought, sinking down and down. Is this what the magician saw in my hand? Or what he only pretended to see? So that he might foretell— And she sank out of view, beneath the queen's chair. In an instant Catherine rose to her feet to announce that the creature had long been ill, that she had insisted on rising from her sickbed to greet the guests with merriment. Finally the queen filled her own goblet from the dwarf's tiny flask and raised it to her lips. Brave Morgantina, she cried. Silence and the fearful drawing of breath descended upon the hall, unfurling like a gathering storm. The queen drained her goblet. Morgantina! echoed the king, and solemnly drained his own. Cornelius followed, and Diane, the king's ministers, at last the guests. The dwarf's name echoed and echoed through the vast hall like a sorcerer's incantation. Then the wine ran like blood from the fountain of life, and the guests fell to a fever of feasting and lechery.

In her far corner of the palace, in the dwarf's quarters, Morgantina lay moaning softly upon silken covers, guarded by four carved silver posts that coiled upward above her bed like plumes of smoke from a dying fire. She heard a ghostly whisper in the corridor; the sound drifted over her gently like a veil, like a devil's familiar calling her name. She reached for her philters, her ampullas, her loathly liquors. Seven Thieves' vinegar? Not to be taken internally. She would have a topaz instead. When swallowed, the topaz relieves melancholy. When placed in the mouth it relieves thirst. Sexual longing is assuaged when it is held on certain parts of the body. Here, she held it; here and here. And yes, even here.

BUT WHAT HAD SICKENED HER? The magician himself? Had he touched her, in her sleep, or was there some waxen image of her, suffering, in his rooms, a thing made from a guttering yellow candle, misshapen as the dwarf herself, its brave light sputtering, perishing? Had he snuffed it out and reshaped it to stand for Morgantina? Was it to be sacrificed in some coward's test? She would not succumb. In her delirium she heard a knocking upon the secret chamber door. The magician appeared. No, she murmured. No.

He had come in charity. He had brought a gift—an

---

impalpable healing powder made from oranges and ambergris, and a certain root gathered on St. John's Eve. But at once she detected another faint odor about him, and began to sniff the air delicately, to uncover its nature. It was strongest on his hands; he gestured as he spoke, causing the fragrance to drift toward her in waves. She held her breath so as not to inhale a poison, if poison it be. Suddenly she knew it—juice of the blue vervain. If he should touch her with his hands; if he should cause this substance to warm her skin and travel to her heart's blood— Bestarbarto entices the inward parts of a woman. Stay away, she hissed. *Faiseur de diables!*

His laughter was a gentle mischief. I—commander of devils? All the court awards that title to Morgantina. Misbegotten child of Basque winds and witches' dreams.

The dwarf folded herself into her famous sleeping knot, so that she could neither see nor hear him more.

You are in pain, he said tenderly. Do not shrink from one who means you well.

She shrank further; her body twisted in upon itself like a sailor's rope. He reached out to her, over her, white hands darting like the heads of snakes. I am this, he murmured, thou are that. That is thou, this is I. Heaven I, Earth thou.

Despite her twisting, despite her clot of limbs and covers, toes blocking her ears, eyes clenched shut against him, the dwarf's body heard and began to loose itself. He chanted on, solemn, oblivious, repeating, circling. I am this, thou art that. He took no notice as she unfolded before him. At last she lay full-stretched, still as a corpse. He stood close enough for her to draw the breath he released. He sent it forth; she drew it in without will, without thought, like one in an enchantment. He touched her in no other way, yet the air between them was a cord of flesh.

Open yourself to me, Morgantina, he said.

Sorcerer, she replied, and spat, and screwed her eyes tighter still.

Sorcery is but an instrument of mind. He spoke as though his words were his hands, stroking her. Pure, shining, subtle vapor . . . He paused to kneel beside her, bowing his head as though in prayer. It rises, he said, from the heart's blood, and is warmed by the heart's own heat . . .

I will not be witched by you. Her voice had the sound of water in her own ears.

Light of eye to light of eye, mind then forming to mind. Open, Morgantina. In this light a god can make worlds vanish.

With an effort that seemed to draw all her feeble strength, the dwarf turned her great head, straining away from him. As she did so, he seized her by the shoulders; he touched her deformity; his greedy fingers closed upon it as though he had captured an enemy treasure. Her eyes flew open and stared, with the gaze of an animal caught at the center of a spreading fire. As his fingers moved over her, she heard him say, Forgive me. There was no need to reply; he had not spoken to her. She remained still, frozen in the moment before his touch. Death. He was her death. With her eyes wide she saw a perfectly white cockerel set upon a circle of letters in the earth; beneath each letter lay a grain of corn. The cockerel began to eat; it pecked first at the grain marked *M*. Then *O*. Then *R*. Morgantina, she thought. Morte, she thought.

Morte, Etam, Tetecame, Zaps, whispered the magician. He had somehow released her limbs from her body; they floated now, stunted arms and legs, elongated, flying, supple and weightless as the air. In water, the shadow of the thing is seen, he said, pressing his warm mouth to her breast. In oil, the appearance of the person. He touched her belly. And in wine—he impaled her, covering her face with his hand—in wine, the very thing itself.

Morgantina screamed; a silence flew from her mouth like a perfectly white cockerel. M—O—R—

The magician touched her lips, his fingers pungent now with an essence she could not recognize, for it was her own.

He was whispering now, his voice thick and urgent. Powdered coral, the womb of a swallow, heart of a dove, blood of a white pigeon mixed with your own . . .

I already know the future, said the dwarf. A child will kill me—

. . . wrap the paste in thin blue silk, enclose it in a ripe green fig, hang it about the neck . . .

Shall I need my wand of poplar wood, half without bark, my bright knife, a pumpkin root?

Cornelius smiled tenderly, and with his fragrant fingers pressed her lips closed. Solemnly he kissed her upon the forehead, that monstrous bulging forehead, and with that kiss he entered into a silent pact with her. Forever after he must cherish her and become at last her protector in all things. Even in all evil things. Perhaps.

THE QUEEN AND HER DWARF are posing for their new portrait. Cornelius is to render Catherine as Athena, Goddess of Wisdom, smiting the Vices of sloth and folly. Morgantina will have two changes of costume, representing these.

Catherine frowns and fidgets. A thousand burnings, she says. I know my cousin; he will hold us to the promise. Righteous murders; heads on spikes. My cousin is a hard and thorough man; he will have his blood price for every pearl in this cursed rope—and proof on it. I swore—

Cornelius lays down his brush. Majesty, he says, adjusting her arm, her head. He will be well satisfied with the closing of a few monasteries; the Brethren will yield up treasure enough from their caves. The king will make much of the burnings. Caskets of gold will prove that his Majesty has restored righteousness in the countryside.

Catherine shakes her head. The Brethren are too small a prize. My cousin believes that all our land is one witch—and that he must not suffer it to live.

Do not frown so, says Cornelius. The Goddess of Wisdom does not frown. Nor a queen who would play her part.

The dwarf, covered with leaves, wearing shoes fashioned like cloven hoofs, has been crouching in Catherine's shadow; now she sends Cornelius a look of loathing. Do you think we have the best artist for this work, Majesty? Or the best magician? He is a foreigner to begin with. We should have been warier.

We had need, says Catherine, of a worthy son of the schools, an amusing chatterer—

A poet skilled in the black arts? Morgantina wears the smile of an imp, to match her costume. A scholar? she says. Able at any moment to quote blasphemies—

All these he certainly is, says Catherine, turning to the light.

And best of all, Morgantina whispers, he is mad.

Look up, Morgantina, says Cornelius, gesturing smoothly with his brush. Tilt the profile toward your mistress—I thought she was to hold the ape in this portrait,

Catherine says. I wanted the ape perched upon my shoulder.

The last ape is dead, says Morgantina. Don't you remember? Poison scraps from the king's table.

Then we need new ones. Why hasn't anyone—my sister promised some for the feast day. Why not wait till then to finish this dreary portrait?

His Majesty wishes the banquet hall completed, madam.

Catherine shrugs. It will do no good. Not the dreadful paintings, the awful jewels. Not the hideous new fortified gates. We cannot show them the one thing they wish to see; therefore we can show them nothing.

Why not show them the dwarf's palm? says Cornelius. The child is there. He turns back to his canvas.

Morgantina has turned pale as ash. The queen whirls sharply to face her. Toad, she says, in a low, pleasant voice. Have you a secret?

The dwarf makes her eyes round and empty. Do not think your magician lacks a heart, she says. This Cornelius is compassionate, full of loving-kindness. He feels pity for a monster who cannot weep, yet must be made to bear a child, and to die from birthing it. He feels pity for a babe whose own mother might smother it in her womb, by a touch, or by her own dying. He pities a poor queen who could love such a babe as her own—unless it be a monster. He pities the king whose virile member fails him, but who would have his queen dragged to the stake by a rope of pearls.

Catherine says nothing, but considers this strange outburst.

The king would have the people on his side, Morgantina goes on. The Pope would not be in the least embarrassed.

Three witnesses would be enough to burn us all, muses the queen. Are not three witnesses readily found—to swear to any lie?

Cornelius smiles. If witnesses are not found in a slanderous court, one can find them in any starving village. When the land is parched, hatred is water, death is fruit and grain.

Morgantina shrugs. And if witnesses are wanting, judges will be content with the general clamor, the public voice. The poor have a potent wail. I have heard it.

There, says Cornelius, with a flourish of sepia from his brush. I have captured the queen smiling.

SINCE THE NIGHT OF THE FEAST Diane has studied the dwarf with her practiced eye. The creature's color is drained and she wears a certain look of fright. Yet Diane has no knowledge of the cause. Is the queen grown more vicious in their game of who can tell? Morgantina's fingers are red and blistered from an orgy of needlework for Catherine's sumptuous new gowns, carefully cut to show her blossoming figure. The dwarf labors silently at menial tasks. She rarely leaves her quarters, and when summoned, she comes with a face full of hate. Visitors now find the sight of her an ill omen, as in ancient days. If one baits her for a jest, asking: What has the swiftest success yet the shortest life? she will not reply, as once she had: Wit. Now she replies, in a voice of ice: Magicians bearing false crowns. No one knows what to make of it. Once, in the queen's salon, a guest asked her for a discourse on witches.

101

If one believes not in witches, the dwarf replied, without smiling, how then in the devil? If not in devils, how then in hell? And without hell, which noble man will do a noble deed?

Cornelius feels her presence in his shadow, as though she has a plan to work him a small harm. He is certain that she creeps into his rooms, seeking a nail paring, or a wisp of hair, to fortify some image of him and work a magic. But he takes care. Any combing of his hair he instantly burns, and he pares his nails over a dark cloth, which he shakes out into the fire. Vexed with her own fears, she takes to rubbing salves into her skin and the membranes of her inward parts, to lose herself in violent dreams.

What is that which flies the swiftest? a guest asks her.
Reason, she replies.
What is the gulf that is never filled? asks another.
The avarice of the rich.
What is most hateful in the young? ventures the queen.
The need for love.
What is most foolish in the old? asks the lady Diane.
Love itself.
What are the things most dangerous in a palace? taunts the king.
Wicked monarchs and the tongues of their servants.

The guests laugh their dangerous laughter. Morgantina folds herself and rolls about the hall like a great jeweled ball.

Once a delighted guest promised to give the dwarf anything she desired. I defy you to do that, she said.
You doubt my good will? said the nobleman.
No. But I aspire to what you do not possess and can never give.

And what is this precious thing?

That which was never in the power of the powerful. It is pleasure.

At last even the queen exploded at her boldness, and kept her confined in the dwarf quarters until her tongue could be controlled.

Morgantina rolled backward out of the royal presence. Remember that a monster is of the nature of a fly, she said. The more you drive her away, the more is she bent to plague you.

Now DIANE WATCHES THE QUEEN with growing suspicion. Is there a true reason for the skillful padding in her new gowns? A real fullness here, a genuine roundness there? Is the faint rosiness in that sallow complexion a result of nature or art? Something is not right. The maidservants in Diane's employ spy upon the queen and swear that her monthly courses have ceased; swear that daily she grows plumper, that her sleep is heavy, her appetites extraordinary. She eats no supper, then sends for sweet cakes and pomegranates in the night. She will see none of the court physicians, but only Cornelius. And he swears that she is with child.

I don't believe it, said Diane. I want to believe it, but I don't.

Henry thought Diane must be deceived by a sudden fit of jealousy. Had not her own artistry wrought this miracle? Had she not sent him from her bed to the queen's— straight and sure as a knight's true arrow? Had not Henry done his manly, his kingly duty? What reasonable doubt was there that they had, between them, got this magic child on Catherine?

At last Diane fell silent, watchful. She would transform her garden, refurbish her salon, destroy the unfinished portraits, order new ones. She resumed her endless correspondence with the great masters of Europe; they must come to paint her, to erect a new statue to Henry. They must design a more glorious fountain, must write a more amusing play; must bring new treasures, toys, animals, books, games, delights. If Catherine would at last assure Henry's crown, then Diane must build his legend, and her own. Three initials are engraved here in marble squares, but the lady Diane may be chiseled away in a fortnight.

DIANE DESCENDS TO THE DWARF'S quarters, to examine the creature. She bends solicitously over the bed.

How do you fare, my little friend? What are all these? She sniffs the oils, infusions, decoctions in vials; the chamber has become a laboratory.

Healing draughts, says Morgantina, avoiding her eyes.

Oil of rue? False unicorn root? You deceive me. All these are plucked from the garden of a woman's desperation.

Morgantina turns her great head, so that her eyes must meet Diane's accusing stare. A dwarf's desperation is unlike that of other women, she says. The queen is with child; she suffers irregularities of the blood, and of the temper. I prepare these remedies for her. It is required that I test them first in case of impurity or disproportion.

Diane studies her. Are you certain about Catherine? She will not see the physicians; why is that?

Certain, madam. The queen is modest and fearful. In her country a woman may shrink from the gaze of all men, even to the time of confinement. She does well to entrust herself only to one.

Diane is unconvinced. But she says only: Great care must be taken; Catherine is a sickly child. And you are ill at the same moment. An odd pair of events.

We must all conspire to guard the queen's health, says Morgantina piously.

Indeed, says Diane. Catherine will need her playmate more than ever. She will take it ill if you—

If I die before her time? And spoil the festal mood? The dwarf's tone is perversely playful. I promise I shall not. For the babe will need me too; Cornelius saw it in my palm. A loyal servant dare not fail so many trusting masters. But how does your moon garden, my lady? And your portrait? The bridge, the banqueting hall, the new poet at the salon? No one tells me anything anymore. They keep me shut up in this dungeon, for fear I will cast a pall.

Diane leans forward and smiles. I must tell you. The frescoes will cause a wonderful scandal. Of course they are dreadful paintings; how could they be otherwise? The man is a bungler. But no one will see anything in the work beyond its delicious immorality. I make a most succulent virgin in the center panel.

Morgantina's smile is a mischief. And the king?

In one corner Henry is portrayed wearing a woman's scarlet gown, and splendid jewels. I think he will adore it, unless I warn him not to. In the center piece—a bacchanal—there are two figures coupling. The artist had to

be very clever there, one must peer quite closely to recognize us. She laughs and claps her hands. O, Morgantina,
it is delicious, wait till you see it.

The dwarf starts. Is there—is there any scene in which
the artist himself can be recognized?

No. I don't think. Unless—wait. There is one corner
in which tiny monsters are seen tormenting each other—
a silly fantasy of hell, I imagine. Cornelius will not let
me study it well—he says it is not yet right. But I did
glimpse—I thought—a strange naked figure holding a
sword with a great crystal pommel.

And a word engraved on it? The letters *A—Z* . . . ?

Letters, yes. I don't remember—perhaps that was it.
A—Z . . . ?

The dwarf shrugged her good shoulder. Who can tell?
What is the strange naked figure doing in the panel?

Diane smiles. He is riding on the naked back of the
king.

Azoth, said Morgantina, in a voice of mock solemnity.
Azoth is the name of Cornelius' demon. He keeps it shut
up in there, in the pommel of his sword.

As soon as any visitor left her, Morgantina sipped
one or another of her tinctures, inducing the violent sickness that must expel the mysterious poison from within
her. Sick she was, and deathly pale, so that even Catherine
appeared to pity her . . . limiting her cuffs and curses to
one a day, after meals. Daily too, the lady Diane came
and perched by the side of her bed, to study the dwarf's
torments and her waking dreams, hoping to find useful
secrets therein.

But there are too many! the dwarf cried aloud, though deep in slumber. How to burn them all?

Who, Morgantina? whispered the lady Diane, bending close to the creature's fevered brow. Who burns?

Mother, replied the dwarf, still sleeping. That one, there; she who stole the child from his grave.

Did she? Truly?

Morgantina's head nodded, though her eyes squeezed tighter shut. The witch confessed it, did you not hear? Though her husband bid them go, and rummage in the grave. The child would be there, he swore, safe, whole, unharmed.

And it was so? They found him?

The dwarf's eyes flew open. You be the judge. Believe the witness of your eyes; trust your hand upon the child's body, or is it a cheat of the devil? A trick of the trickster? We are all deceived; therefore burn them.

Diane sighed and shook her head. In time of trouble, some do prefer the confession to the fact.

Is she burnt yet? Morgantina hissed, sinking back into her troubled sleep. Here is a maiden, swears she coupled with the devil. Yet she is proved a maiden still. How can it be? Another cheat! Burn her. Look—she is in a great hurry; she longs for the fire; she burns for it. Why did she tell the lie? Her lie? Theirs? Her madness? Yours?

Diane leans forward. Are you with child, Morgantina? Is it Henry's? Will you not trust me? Once you did. I will protect you, I swear it. Is it the king's child?

Morgantina's stricken eyes now blaze with a sudden sly clarity. It is the queen's, she said, leaving Diane to ponder.

Daily thereafter Diane kept her watchful silence, as the queen's robes billowed out, as her breasts swelled and rounded, her cheeks burst into sudden rosy bloom. Joyful

107

whispers flew about the court, accompanied by the ringing of bells, the lighting of candles, the chanting of prayers. The Pope sent three great chests of carved white holly wood filled with bars of gold. The king ordered work to resume on fortifications, fountains, magnificent new gates. A round of new feast days permitted the people to rejoice by offering gifts of gold and jewels. Promises of useful things came from foreign lands: marriages, treasures, armies, friendships. It was a time of shimmering hope.

DIANE AND HENRY CELEBRATE in their own way, with new wine and familiar kisses. The lady toasts her lord:

So, my love, success is ours. Catherine looks quite radiant, don't you agree? She was born for this hour.

Henry's doubts persist, even in the soft bed of his mistress. What if she fails, if it dies, if she dies?

O, Henry, she chides him, we have come so far. Can we not rejoice for a minute? Seven years of barrenness, followed by seven fat babies. Seven at least—I promise you. One for every throne in Christendom. Catherine's womb will spring open like a casket, spilling treasure. You have only to love me well. I will always send you, full of your kingly powers, to get your pretty children on her.

Still the king tosses and twists. She will have no physician tend her—only Cornelius.

That is wise. He has a calming power.

I thought we agreed that he is odious. A sorry painter, a fraud—

Diane nods. —Indifferent rhymester, profligate, spendthrift. Even his festal decorations are shoddy. Nothing he does is half so good as the paintings he makes with his boasting. But I concede that his palm readings are of some amusement—

Henry's frown darkens. The man is a thorough rascal. I trust him not.

Nor I, says Diane smoothly. The worst of his breed we have yet engaged. Still, Catherine dotes on him—

I wonder why she does.

What? Diane turns to study him. Jealous? I do believe you are. This little queen is more to your liking now? Is it so?

Don't tease me, Diane. But she is improved. Her disposition—

Her bosom? Well, if you are grown jealous, then so shall I. Yes. I am already.

Henry is used to this. Catherine is queen and wife, he says, defensively. Diane is love and life. Must I forever reassure you? Can I ever?

Diane laughs with wry pleasure, ticking off her fingers. Are the crown jewels in my care? My portrait as the Madonna, does it yet hang in the royal chapel? Have I a sweet palace of my own—a lovely white one in the south, for instance, which the crown has lately accepted from that poor banker, what was his name?

Henry laughs with her. I fear my love grows greedy as the queen grows fat.

Don't blame me, Henry. When you and Catherine are dandling little princes, I will have need of refuge, and money, and proof of your love. Well you know how Catherine delights in the thought of my absence. As soon as the child comes—

The king embraces her. Catherine owes you much. And the little prince—if there be one—owes you his life.

_____

Diane's smile is rueful. A debt may be owed; acknowledging it—paying it—is another matter. Especially for kings and queens.

Henry licks his dry lips. As to the portrait, I promised you that honor long ago. It shall be my gift of thanks on the day of the child's birth. A fitting tribute to his true mother—and mine. Now will you kiss me?

She will kiss him. O, she will.

Never leave me, he murmurs, growing kingly beneath her practiced hands.

Never, she says, until death.

BUT BY DAY THE KING'S DOUBTS multiply, and by night his fears overtake him. Soon even Diane's touch fails. On a desperate whim, he summons the magician.

How does the queen? he asks, as though this is the reason for their meeting.

Cornelius is smooth and skillful. She blooms, sire, as her garden does. One seldom sees so delicate a child take to a woman's state with such a natural ease.

Henry is embarrassed; he fidgets; he avoids the magician's gaze. Does she have need of medicines? Of special foods? Tonics? We could send—

No, sire, says Cornelius. All goes well.

Good, then; good. But how goes all our other business—portraits, fountains, medals, gates, horoscopes, library? Cataloguing of gifts from the queen's journey? And, ah, the dwarf? How fares the creature—

All well, sire. Morgantina needs rest. The portraits need time. The counting of new treasure is nearly done;

I think your Majesty will be well satisfied. Cornelius pauses, draws a breath. Ah—perhaps some payment may be made for the workmen? To the purveyors of silver for the doors, or the stonecutters? You have seen the magnificent block of marble. The lady Diane has chosen well.

Yes, says Henry, absently. Yes; good. We will see to it.

Cornelius bows, makes a gesture of withdrawal.

Wait. Henry lowers his voice to a conspirator's tone. I have heard that you treat the sickness of night fears; of failure of the virile member. One of our ministers, one of our knights, a nobleman of high rank—

Cornelius smiles. Send the man to my laboratory, sire. I will be honored to attend him.

The king's eyes shift again. Good. That is all, then.

Cornelius withdraws to his rooms, to await his visitor.

Henry appears, in a cloak of disguise, borrowed from an aide of his chamber. Cornelius expresses no surprise, but gestures toward the table upon which the man must lie. The magician snuffs out all candles save one. Henry climbs upon the table, stretches out, closes his eyes. Cornelius grasps a royal ankle between two fingers. At a single point, he presses the fingers together as though he would snap the bone like a dry twig. The king does not cry out. The magician presses harder still. Tell me, he says, if it is a sore point.

The king gasps. It was not; but now it may be.

Cornelius relaxes his hold, and seizes the foot itself. What of this?

111

Now the magician moves swiftly, seizing in turn knees, long bones of the thighs, hips, shoulders. Now he rests a hand lightly upon the royal pelvis, lifts it, pauses at the center as though to measure the temperature of air rising from the virile member. The king begins to sweat. Cornelius thrusts a finger into the royal ears and presses, as though to make them meet. Henry's throat closes; he would cry out now if he could. The magician commences to speak. Once upon a time, he says, in a voice so soft as to seem a whisper, yet with sound and rhythm, as a poet speaks his poem, a race of men, quaint, venturesome, and fabulously bold, left many widows, from their habit of sailing out into the roughest seas to hunt for creatures of the deep: Sciapods and narwhal, the horse and the star. They sailed out, leaving their wives to God or the devil . . .

Henry lies rigid, his eyes tight shut, listening. The hands and voice of Cornelius drift over him, sending currents of air and sound like waves of water.

. . . as for their children, the magician went on, in his liquid song, these honest worthy men of the sea would have thought more about them if they had been clear as to who their fathers were . . . But on their return home, each sailor reckoned up the months of his journey . . . and somehow he never found the reckoning right.

Henry felt an involuntary shuddering in his limbs. The magician's voice ceased, but still his hands hovered like birds, like white rooks, somewhere over the king's body. With his eyes closed, Henry could not tell exactly where the hands were, where the man was. Yet he did not open his eyes; he knew not why.

Return from the sea, sire, Cornelius said. The air was suddenly chill; the magician had withdrawn.

Henry opened one cautious eye; the chamber where

he lay was empty and dark but for the single quivering candle at his feet. A vial of shimmering amber liquid stood beside him on a small table. He rose trembling, conscious of a shameful heat at the center of his body, a sweet tremor in the legs; for an instant he doubted they would support him. At last he stood, swaying on his feet. What had the man done to him? Cornelius awaited him, just outside the door. Take this, he said, pressing a pale rough crystal into the king's hands. Its points sparkled like danger. Set it in a warm bath this night. Enjoy your lady's company, but not her bed.

The king made no reply, but swept past the man, mustering his dignity, gathering his cloak. Confused images flickered in his mind. Sirens sporting in roiling seas, women with swollen bellies and flame-colored hair. Diane naked, wearing the Virgin's halo; Catherine weeping, Cornelius laughing, the dwarf muttering curses in an unknown tongue.

The magician's voice trailed behind him softly, like a train of velvet: Rest well. And softer still: Majesty.

MORGANTINA'S STRENGTH IS RESTORED; it must be; she wills it to be. She weeps with her hands over her face, as always; none ever saw that she shed no tears. In her sleep she has heard a continuous lovely singing, a rhythmic humming without words, that rises and falls, and rises again. She wakes with the sound echoing still, rising, falling. She wakes with the moving of her body, though she herself has not moved; a beating upon her inmost self, like the drumming of a prisoned heart. She lies perfectly still, watching her belly rise up against her like a menacing

---

stranger; it hardens into a knot of flesh, a fist, a hump like the other, only alive; kicking. Slowly she moves her own knotted fists over the spot, covering it, pressing down upon it; perhaps the thing will choke inside her, she thinks. Perhaps it will turn, twisting until its own cord of life tightens about its own neck and strangles it. It was the way Morgantina's own sisters, and the brother who came before her, all died inside their bold, beautiful mother. That mother who mothered not, who shut Morgantina up in her dwarfing cage and spent her days seated on a tomb in the graveyard, laughing with her friends, shaking their gleaming hair, whispering their secrets. They ran to the sea, and danced there, like fish. They ran to the forest and danced there, like devils. Silly wretched girls who went to dance, and whisper, swearing never to bear a child. They lived from day to day on a handful of coins from their labors, their sewing, their scrubbing. They lived for the Sabbath feasts of barrenness in their forest, for love without love, a devil's kiss that would bear no fruit, no life to drain their own. In the forests they found fruits of another kind, wild berries glistening with magic juices. Rubbed upon their lips, their bodies, until their eyes filled with pretty dreams—theaters and beautiful gardens; until their wretched fingers seemed to touch silver ornaments and gowns full of twinkling light; until handsome youths seemed to dance with them, and music to play, and noblemen to kiss their hands. Captive silly girls who danced and feasted and dreamed with a fierce and terrible urgency, lest they wake and find themselves with child. Morgantina's mother, captive silly girl, living for pretty dreams, burning for them, being burnt for them, happy to go, in a great haste. As though in the fire, a dreamer became her dream.

Morgantina closes her eyes again; she would flee into an endless sleep. She does not hear Cornelius enter, crouching, bending low, as all must who enter the dwarf's quarters. In better times, Morgantina laughed to see such giants shrink, taking such pains to dwarf themselves. She starts as he approaches her. Get away from me! Away...

Morgantina, he pleads tenderly. You must let me tend you. Must know I will not let you die.

Have you come to paint me first, with my double hump? Look, it rises to your summons. Your familiar!

He reaches toward her, but she rolls over upon her belly, gasping with the effort. Die, she whispers. Die now. Hurry.

It is a magical child, he says. His voice is soft, beseeching. It has both our magics, mixed. It shall never harm you or me.

She does not answer.

The table beside her is littered with empty vials, trails of powder, a stone mortar thick with the remains of some foul paste, unguents. He touches these things with a cautious fingertip, smells them, tastes them, grimaces. She turns her head just enough to follow his movements with baleful eyes.

I shall destroy the thing first, she says. You know that I will find the way.

Not with these sorry remedies. He laughs, but keeps his voice gentle. The child is meant to survive. You must believe I mean you no harm.

Then tell the king! she cries. He will destroy it for me. He will not suffer it to live.

No, says the magician. You will bear it bravely until the hour of its birth, in the queen's own childbed. You will send it forth as you have borne it, without a cry. And if it be perfect, you will care for it. All this is in your hand. All honor will be yours, in a prosperous time.

And if it be a monster? Like me or, worse, like you? And if it be a child of the least normal size, to kill me in the bargain?

If it grow too large, I will cut it free without harming you. I swear it, Morgantina. I am a doctor. Only trust me in all things. All will be well for us. I am with you. Drink this instead of that. Eat what is provided. Ease his journey, and your own. This is a time for rejoicing; between us we shall save the king's honor. The queen will reward us richly.

Morgantina laughs, a harsh and bitter sound. Now I know you are mad. If the child kills me not, in the hour of its wretched birth, if I am not split in two, like a heretic put to the saw—why then the queen will thank us both for our trouble with a hasty burning, lest our tongues give up the truth of this business.

I will keep you safe, Morgantina. On my life and yours. You must believe it. You must.

Morgantina's body has grown so great that she can no longer fold up into her famous sleeping posture, forcing the world to be silent. She can only roll this way or that; she can only open her eyes or close them. She closes them now. Death, she says, I knew you from the first.

The magician has moved silently to the foot of her bed; he stretches out his white hands and holds them apart, above her body, as though he bears an invisible treasure, a Morgantina of air. If you could wish it gone, you would not, he says suddenly, in a tone of surprise. That is why you have failed to rid yourself of it with these poisons.

She hesitates; then, in a halting voice, harsh with pain like her laughter, she says: My mother killed her own mother from within her belly, in the hour of her birth. My mother killed my sisters and brother, each in turn, lest they do the same to her. I was never meant to be as I am. I was never meant to be at all.

But you are, Cornelius says gently.

She forces open her eyes; she forces them to meet his. She has a sudden thought that twists her mouth into a smile. I will not try anymore to kill it. Only stay away from me. Unless I call for you. And I will not.

He stiffens. But—as you wish, then. You will rest? You will eat what is prepared for you? And the tonics—

Attend the queen, Cornelius. Attend her well. The dwarf's voice rings with authority. She closes her eyes again, and lies perfectly still, listening to the echo of his retreat. Then she rises, a great misshapen ball; she cannot see her feet, but she propels them, by force of will, to her wardrobe, within which she stores her unfinished secret paintings, rolled up inside discarded rugs and tapestries that the queen has tired of or replaced with more valuable treasures. With resolute calm she takes up her brushes, her palette. Time is short; she must paint directly with the brush now, sketching with burnt umber, dark to light, wet into wet, surfaces that reflect and deflect; glistening coins, vessels of gleaming brass, glasses that magnify or reduce, transient bubbles that distort, that reveal, enigmatic images that are, or are not, dwarf, queen, king, mistress, magician. She must make the color brilliant, more brilliant still, so brilliant that all must wonder what unearthly light shone upon it at the moment of her touch.

She must paint faster, must complete what she has begun, while there is yet time. The creature stirs within her, as if it would speak its threat, its warning. Yes, she says to it, tenderly. I know.

117

CATHERINE DESCENDS TO the dwarf's quarters; a rare visit. She darts about the chamber, agitated, fingering the tiny treasures—the carving of Salome dancing, her veils unfurling, the head of the Baptist, all in minutest detail, upon a peach stone. The painting of a witch trial, with every infinitesimal nail visible in the prisoner's flesh; the rack and the wheel drawn precisely to scale—and the entire picture so small it could be covered by half an ear of wheat.

Presently the queen stops before the dwarf's bed. And so, little beauty, she says, God has heard your most fervent wish—and it is granted.

My wish?

Catherine laughs. Your wish to be enlarged. To be granted largesse. To be puffed up. To achieve greatness! She leans forward to pinch the dwarf's belly. Morgantina smiles wearily. But how little you reveal, even now, says Catherine.

Morgantina sighs, lowers her gaze. The queen's creature may reveal no more than her mistress chooses to perceive.

Is that a jest? Catherine snaps. You can ill afford it. *Was* it the king who ravished you? He denies it. And I believe him. I choose to. In fact, I choose not to know the fact. I choose that Henry not know the fact that I choose at all. We perceive that I am with child; that satisfies us all.

All, says Morgantina, save one.

The queen is toying with her golden darning needle,

her silver-gilt sewing shears. The blades are poised, glittering. She lays them delicately in her lap. Save one? she echoes. I cannot imagine one to be saved. Is one worth saving? She sighs, elaborately. These days one is never sure.

Who can tell? whispers Morgantina, respectfully. The ending is subject to change.

The queen frowns. Jesting again? Yes, she decides, and reconsiders her earlier decision not to strike. With one hand, she rolls Morgantina over; with the other she thrusts the needle into the creature's buttock, so as not to disturb the business in front. The dwarf makes a wincing face, yelping though she feels no pain through her layers of armor. She is laced now, fore and aft, so tight that, when she stands, nothing of her condition can be discerned. Cornelius has assured himself that this will not harm the babe; indeed, that it will be well protected, though Morgantina herself can scarcely breathe, and often swoons with the effort of walking, speaking, or swallowing food.

HENRY LIES WITH THE LADY DIANE; she has kept him with her a night and a day, as in the earliest time of their love. She sighs; they must rise now, breaking the mood. We have promised to meet with Cornelius in the banqueting hall. He is waiting. In truth she has had him wait since noon, in part to cause him anxiety, in part to make his paintings look poorer in the fading light. I want you to look at what he has said about us, on the walls.

You hate it? says Henry, though he is not much interested.

It is not for me to hate or not hate, but for you to decide how you wish the world to see us.

Some who have seen it say it is brilliant.

Diane smiles. Some assume we will think so. You seem to find no fault with Cornelius. Therefore they seek to praise him first. It is the disease of courtiers.

Henry looks puzzled. Do I find fault with him?

Diane embraces him, pulls at his earlobe, laughs. Dearest Henry, you are a generous, patient, forgiving master. And I love you for it. That fellow has completed nothing of worth in all the time we have kept him.

Henry ponders this. The fellow does complain. He says he cannot complete things if we do not pay his debts. I gave him what silver I had for the fountain, and bronze for the great doors. But he said there was not enough of either. And he paid the stonecutter out of his own pocket—

Out of my pocket, says Diane. And the queen's. You see. She gestures, helplessly.

I thought you were pleased with the portrait, at least.

She makes a face. He has given me the head of Medusa.

Henry smiles. Perhaps you gaze at him as she would.

Diane stiffens. I don't gaze at him at all. Are you not troubled by how the queen dotes on him?

The queen always troubles me.

She does not trouble Cornelius.

Henry looks at her sharply. You would not suggest—

No, says Diane, tugging at his other earlobe. I would not suggest.

But you find the attachment unseemly?

I? Diane's eyes widen. I—cast stones about what is seemly? I find it merely dangerous. And with that, she slides gracefully out of the king's encircling arms. Look, it is growing dark. Let us see what slander the man has put on our walls.

In the great banqueting hall, Cornelius paces, watching the light fade. He fusses with candles, hangs panels of gauze veiling over certain parts of the work, moves statues, torches, easels. Now he squints at each section of the great mural, gauging the play of light and shadow upon it, moving candelabra about, lighting this taper, extinguishing that, to illumine the best points, as the most glaring faults recede. The images appear to move, eerily, as he manipulates them. It is a trick of the light; he smiles. Again he adjusts a wisp of veiling, covering the genitals of one figure, the face of another.

A drumbeat of footsteps echoes from both ends of the marble corridor: Diane's end of the gallery, the palace. Quickly he steps back to the center of the hall, turning away from the glowing walls, so as to appear calm, indifferent, gazing outward through an archway, contemplating the shining river; rising white moon sliced by jagged branches; the queen's dark garden, Diane's pale luminous one beside it; looming shrubs of the geometric maze; gleaming statues of ancient heroes; unfinished fountain; rough stone wall behind which the dwarf tended her secret crops—

Cornelius. It is the voice of the queen. The dwarf Morgantina is with her, upon her, dangling from her. In the dancing torchlight, the creature's eyes shine as they had on the first night she came before him, leaping like a dangerous fire, flinging her cloak above her head, dis-

121

playing her monstrous naked limbs, her grotesque whiteness, her power. She is swollen now, distended with life or with death; her gown, like Catherine's, the color of pomegranate, scarlet fruit for a queen of hell.

Queen and dwarf gaze in silence upon the shimmering walls. Noblemen, courtiers, attendants strain forward for a signal, smile, frown, twitch of eye or lip, shrug of shoulder; shall there be praise, faint or thunderous, a cutting word, anger, fury? Is the work sorry, fine, magnificent?

Henry and Diane stand encircled by another troop of attendants. Diane whispers into the king's ear. Move the candles; one cannot see the work for the tricks of eye played by light.

Cornelius obeys; he is well prepared. As the lights move, a host of new images spring forth to the eye. In spite of themselves courtiers stand transfixed, forgetful of the need to study instead the mood of their masters.

In the daylight, says Diane, it will have none of these effects. It will lie flat, dull, and dark, the figures tangled in lifeless heaps—

Look there, Henry whispers back. Is that supposed to be me?

The dwarf gasps. In every detail, this section of the work is hers, magnified to grotesque size, distorted by a heavy brush, dripping red ocher against cold gray. There is the king naked, ridden by the magician, whose sword lies buried, up to its crystal pommel, in the king's posterior. The letters AZOTH are plain to see. And there the lady Diane lies coupled—no, tripled—with king and magician, with dwarf and queen. Familiar faces, noblemen and priests, appear everywhere, upon creatures that fly and crawl, or hide amid leafy branches, or burrow in the earth, eyes glinting like gemstones.

Henry moves closer to the central panel, peering at the image of a fountain that seems made of living flesh. Diane whispers again. What is he hiding with those wisps of gauze?

Remove the veils, Henry commands.

At a touch, the gauze panels float downward, each in turn, revealing genitals and faces of all the court: noble ladies and gentlemen, bankers, foreign princes, the Pope himself.

Catherine pales; Diane reddens; Henry smiles. The dwarf fastens her black gaze upon Cornelius, as if it were a curse.

Perhaps it will be less . . . confusing in the light of day, after all, says Catherine, and turns on her heel. Morgantina scurries after her, though her swollen face still twists backward, eyes still fixed upon the magician.

Perhaps, yes. Henry nods, licking his dry lips. Meanwhile, his eyes devour every vivid inch of the wall.

Murmurs of shock and titillation eddy about the hall like ripples of charged water after lightning.

We can always have it painted over, Diane whispers. Before the archbishop hears of it.

Your Majesty is pleased? says Cornelius, with a confident smile.

You shall be amply rewarded, Henry replies, in a careful tone. Beyond your dreams. Diane lifts her black sleeve; its white slashes gape as she moves toward the king.

The magician bows. The hall empties. For a moment Cornelius stands alone with his work. It is monstrous, he says aloud, to no one. A monster piece. Like the dwarf.

CATHERINE IS PACING RESTLESSLY in her red salon. The dwarf sits, silent, bent over a delicate drift of lace. It is an exquisite pattern of butterflies caught in a fine, almost invisible, web.

Moistening the thread with your horrid tongue? says the queen suddenly. Look—you have ruined it! See the dark patch, there? Your spit is poison. In my father's kingdom only a madwoman would let you touch a skein of such a garment.

Morgantina says nothing to this outburst. Catherine seizes the delicate thread and pulls; one exquisite butterfly vanishes, and another. A month's work. Two.

Morgantina sighs. It will not be finished in time, Majesty.

Catherine plucks at the cloth with her scissors, her fingers, her furious rage. In an instant the lovely border is destroyed; then the cloth itself. Threads fly like blown dandelions. Three years' work for thirty skilled needlewomen. See what you have done! Catherine shrieks.

Morgantina gives her skirt a shake; the ravelings of her beautiful work tumble off her lap, flying like flakes of snow, like crumbs of a teacake. Your Majesty's mood lightens when the magician attends you, she says quietly. The queen refuses to be distracted. Did you see how he slandered me on that wall? she cries. He is a viper, like you.

Morgantina shrugs, though in truth even this tiny gesture is now accomplished only with great effort. I thought the queen looked radiant in the center panel, she muses. Lovely breasts veiled in transparent gauze. One was reminded of the legend of that emperor's wife, as the ancients painted her.

Really? Which emperor? The queen fingers her scissors, deciding whether the dwarf is sincere.

Caesar? ventures the dwarf. Caligula?

The shears flash: snip, snap. Morgantina, no longer nimble, rolls hastily to the floor, not quite in time. Her left ear is cropped and the left arm sheared off at the shoulder, dangerously close to the hump. It is a nasty mess; the queen must step lively to avoid a spattering.

Fortunately, these daily tantrums have already caused the ripping and shredding of all the precious lacework for the baby's christening robes, bonnet, carrying cushion, and receiving blanket. Otherwise, the dwarf would be severely punished for such a copious shedding of blood.

As it is, that ear and arm will require careful stitching with exceedingly fine silk thread, and many days' painful rest in the dwarf's quarters. A creature in Morgantina's delicate condition will not heal as readily as one who is not already in mortal danger from carrying a full-sized child.

In truth, Catherine's rage is the magician's doing, and not Morgantina's at all. The dwarf knows this well, for it was she who set the stage for it this day: A single magnificent pearl, of immense size, bound by an almost invisible thread, placed in the pocket of Cornelius' coat, and a hole, artfully cut in that pocket, so that, as the magician hovered over the queen, as she lay upon her bed, as he murmured his soothing words, as he passed his white hands to and fro, fro and to, at that hushed moment, both sacred and profane, the dwarf, well hidden within a mouse hole in another chamber, holding the almost invisible thread, pulled it gently, causing the great pearl to drop through the pocket and roll noisily upon the marble floor. The dwarf reeled in her invisible thread; the pearl rolled and rolled like a clap of thunder, so that the queen started out of her sleep that was not sleep, and turned in fright toward the rude sound, and stared at the marvelous glowing pearl.

125

Pearl? How came it to be there? This pearl, this pearl was one of hers, she knew it; it belonged to her precious rope, her Pope's rope. But the rope was perfect, no pearl was lacking. Had he then forged it? Replaced a true pearl with a false? A conjurer's cheat, a treason? How many other pearls had he stolen thus? How many other treasures, treasons, treacheries?

She gazed at him in disbelief, in accusation. He stammered and stumbled. He knew not how this came to pass, this pearl, this pearl. What thief may seek to discredit him, Cornelius? What villain would shatter the queen's trust in her faithful servant? How could he, why would he, how could she doubt his stainless honor?

Catherine sank back upon her cushions, closed her eyes, retreated into her furious thoughts. Her body remained tense, rigid, alert. Cornelius held the casket of empty air above her, moved it here, there, here again. She did not soften. She did not yield. It was the first time that he offered her his healing gift, and her body refused it.

HENRY IS WALKING ALONE in the garden maze, stroking his smooth dark stone for company, for comfort. Diane has left him in a mood of dis-ease. Ordinarily she is careful to avoid this, lest others seize the moment to further their own causes. But today she must absent herself for an hour: there are emissaries from abroad, seeking favors; a very great artist has proposed a portrait; and a poet, who has composed a magnificent ode to her beauty, wishes only to present it to the king.

Cornelius enters the maze by another path; he has been

waiting for such a moment; they will meet by chance, and by surprise. The magician too has a gift for the king; it is a fine notion to seize Henry's fancy, dispel his melancholy, and enrich his treasury, all in a single bold stroke. If the plan succeeds, Cornelius may leap over the wall of Diane's hatred, and Catherine's, and the dwarf's, into a safe and honored place by the king's side, forever.

It is a simple scheme. Not ten days' ride from the palace lies a small village, through which Cornelius once passed on his travels from one duchy to another. In the village he heard a tale of evil and of treasure that he savored and held to himself, awaiting this fortunate time.

For just beyond that village, in a valley hidden by two hills in the shape of dwarf's humps, lies a pure spring whose waters flow together, forming a tricorn lake, blue and clear as a liquid sapphire. The waters of this spring are much worshipped by the older peasants; they call it the Source, and believe that it possesses healing powers. At the topmost point of the Source dwells a band of heretics called the Brethren of the Free Spirit.

In the nearby villages it is said that these Brethren have amassed a wealth of treasure through gold and silver mined from the hills around them, and perhaps stolen from neighboring towns. Yet these Brethren, fugitives from other lands, have never paid their taxes to the king, much less brought gifts on the appropriate feast days. Indeed, it is said that, on such days, instead of paying homage to their sovereign, and the Church, the Brethren celebrate their own unholy beliefs, in strange rituals, in an underground cavern filled with treasure. They pray before a magnificent altar, upon which are arrayed their icons, images of naked devils and fornicators, all finely wrought of silver-gilt and gold. The ceremonies themselves are or-

gies of such perversity, such blasphemy, such unimagin-
able acts of bestiality and defilement that Cornelius' own
ears, cropped as they are for his own heresies, blushed to
hear of them.

Now from behind a screen of shrubbery he fills the
ears of the king, embroidering and embellishing where he
must, like a court painter who bedecks his subject with
jewels and fine lace. Had Henry never heard the tales of
human sacrifice, of the eating of infant flesh, of the drain-
ing of blood—all going on in the very shadow of proper
Christian communities, villages filled with decent, law-
abiding souls? Were not these righteous, simple folk in
mortal danger? Had not the moment now come for their
king to deliver them from this plague of devils? Could he
afford to stay his hand, while fiends and whoremasters
robbed and plundered the rightful treasure of the crown?

Are they armed? says Henry, his face still hidden behind the hedgerow. Though the shrubbery screens the king
from his direct gaze, Cornelius marks well the king's excited tone, the eager lightening of his step. Only with the
devil's fork, the magician replies, with a voice of certainty,
of measured calm.

Henry grips his stone; it slips from his fingers; he
retrieves it quickly from the graveled path. What about
fortifications?

None, sire. They believe in the protection of the harsh
landscape, and their blasted faith.

A certain change occurs in Henry's voice; a quaver of
doubt. You have seen them—this place—with your own
eyes?

Indeed, sire. Cornelius lies with smooth lips. It hangs
like a poisonous peach ripening upon your own tree; if
your hand but extends, it must fall to you, with a prayer

128

of thanks from all the people, from the Church, from God Himself.

How many men would we need?

Scarce a hundred soldiers, sire, good riders all, and bearers to carry out the treasure. They need not ride back through the village. Why stir the greed of good towns-people who have lived so long near this mouth of hell? Melt down the vile statues and relics; you'll have enough silver to finish the gates, the fountain, the eastern forti-fications. Enough gold to repay your creditors, equip the new army—

You're certain they're not armed?

Certain, Majesty.

Gold? How do you know?

Cornelius springs forth from behind his fence of shrub-bery. In his hands he holds a magnificent object: a pair of enormous gold satyrs flanking a silver-gilt mirror that is shaped like a goblet, ornamented with a devil's face, and the words *Morte, Etam, Tetacame, Zaps*. It is a piece of extraordinary workmanship; the king gapes at it, awe-struck, as though it were alive with devilish power.

From their altar, Majesty, whispers the magician, stroking it. Hold it so, facing the surface of any liquid. Truth will appear, or a devil incarnate. Depending.

Henry shrinks back. How came you by it?

In trade, says Cornelius. In truth he has fashioned the icon with the king's own silver and gold; its design is a faithful copy of an ancient altarpiece, an engraving of which Cornelius recently discovered in a rare text about devil worship. (The manuscript itself he stole from among the queen's new store of treasures.) The original altar-piece, captured by soldiers of the papal army in the hills of a distant country, is thought to have disappeared centuries ago, when a tribe of pagan worshippers was destroyed by fire and sword, their dwelling places sacked, their treasure seized for the papal coffers.

We cannot equip such an expedition, Henry says. No one will lend us the money. All the queen's treasure has raised scarcely enough to pay our old debts and finish the eastern gate.

Cornelius appears to ponder this: his expression is grave, thoughtful. A troop of mercenaries? he says presently. Would the Church not help us? Would not the archbishop take a lively interest in flushing out this richly lined pocket of the devil? Would he not seek the Holy Father's blessing? Would he withhold it?

I'd have to tell him about the treasure, says Henry. He would want—

Ah, Cornelius nods, sagely. It is only right and natural that the poison fruits be washed by the Holy Father's own hands. Before—

Henry bridles at this; Cornelius knew he would. Turn it all over to the Church? Risk good men to fill Clement's bulging treasury? Are you mad?

The magician restrains a gleeful, unseemly laughter. If I may suggest, Majesty, good men must be sacrificed or the treasure will never reach us. You. The Pope must be assured of his portion, in addition to his share of the glory for our triumph. We must invade this foul place in the name of Holy Church, lest it be painted by evil slanderers as royal banditry and plunder. These Brethren, these free spirits, have lived in peace in the countryside; they have seemed harmless to many. In time of plenty, their neighbors grumble not, nor make any claim of trespass.

Well, can't we get some of them to complain first? Dig

---

up an infant's grave or something? The bishops prefer a nice clean witchcraft case, with a friendly town to cheer the burnings.

Again Cornelius nods. The town is ripe for friendliness, sire. As for burnings, hungry peasants are not above scavenging. Well-fed strangers are the devil's friends, are they not? Else whence comes their treasure, in such troubled times? If not by black art, then how? How do fiends fatten, except on the bodies and souls of innocents?

That is true, says Henry, still in a wavering tone. I will think on it. But Cornelius sees that he is feverish now with greed, with the possibilities of easy picking. The lady Diane will like the idea well, says the magician. He has been saving this persuasion for last.

Henry is startled; he flushes. You spoke of this to her?

I would not presume, sire. But this I know: she yearns to bring a certain master painter here, for her new portrait. And a great sculptor from the East, as well, for your Majesty's equestrian statue. She loves not my poor efforts for these great works. And in simple truth, she is right. The magician pauses, measuring the impact of his cleverness. He is rewarded; Henry shakes his head in loyal protest. No, no, insists Cornelius, gesturing. She is right. No mere Cornelius can do justice to the lady's surpassing charm. Yet without some new fortune, the masters will not come. The lady's ambition—

Henry stiffens. The lady's ambition is for this court.

Of course it is, says Cornelius. For the glory of your Majesty. And rightly so! She has an exquisite sensibility, a refinement, a brilliant eye. She will not rest until the sun gathers all of its rays upon the crown that is Henry's.

That is so, says Henry, mollified.

This venture I propose would be but a small beginning.

Yet I flatter myself to imagine she will delight in such a triumph for you, no less than in the spoils you will lay at her feet. Especially in this time, while the queen gathers praise for her newfound fecundity, and the lady Diane, for all her brilliance, languishes for lack of both.

You see much, magician.

I am proud to keep watch for so wise and bold a master, says Cornelius, adding a bow and a flourish.

I will think hard upon it.

Not long, though, sire. There are other ears in those mountain villages. Thieves abound. Plunderers.

Henry smiles. Thieves and plunderers not protected by holy laws—

—Nor by the righteous wrath of their king.

At this, the king turns abruptly, to get out of the maze by the way he came. For an instant he is confused.

Here is the way, says Cornelius, bowing again, retreating along his own sure pathway.

Henry nods, straightens up, recovers his stride, follows the magician into the clearing. Outside the shadowed hedgerows, the sudden sun is blinding; Henry hesitates, then hastens off in the direction of Diane's white garden, where she awaits him. Shall he tell her at once of his meeting with the magician, of their discourse? No, he decides. He will wait to surprise her, after he has approved the plan. He will show her, for once, that he can act with boldness. Alone. Decisively. Manly; kingly; godly. He imagines her tender smile. How proud she will be. Bold Henry. Heart of the lion, head of the eagle. How sweetly she will embrace him, grateful for his promises. Yes. It is done.

CATHERINE SITS ENTRANCED before the triptych, as some women sit before the looking-glass: her lips are parted, her breath light and rhythmic, as Cornelius has instructed her. In this way she enters the central panel, her favorite of the three, with its strange fountain of flesh that bears both fruit and water flowing in transparent crystal arcs. Its luminous naked figures seem to spring up from the ground like wildflowers; their faces bear no more shame, no more guile or cunning, than the faces of the birds and four-footed creatures that surround them. If the magician is to be believed, this painted place is not in heaven, not in the fevered imagination of a madman, but here, in her own kingdom. The people are real, alive, hidden nearby in the very hills beyond this palace. She could find them if she wished, if she dared. She could join their fellowship for a night or a day; undertake a secret journey, in disguise. A fortnight's absence, pleading the privilege of her delicate state; a visit to some convent of nursing sisters. Daily her dreams are invaded by such thoughts; her desire, her fever grow stronger. Does Cornelius truly know where the Brethren hide? Is he to be trusted? If not, how shall the trickster be tricked?

At last, the plan comes to her whole. She will make a pilgrimage to the abbey near Saint Pé, to spend the fortnight in prayer and rest, for her health, for the health of the child. She will be cared for by the good abbess and the Sisters, nourished by simple fare and pure mountain water. She will take the dwarf for company. Henry will be easily persuaded; Diane will be delighted by her going. Catherine wrests her gaze from the glowing images before her and gazes out of her window. Diane's garden blooms anew, all in a sudden cavalcade of yellow and indigo, tall spires of hollyhock and lupine, guarding the tousled, clustered hydrangea that nod in the breeze like gossips' heads. For this fortnight, Diane will have both gardens, and the court, and all of Henry. Catherine permits herself a tiny, secret smile. For the last time, perhaps.

HENRY HAS RETIRED to Diane's bedchamber, where she awaits him with a lively fire, wine, a cold supper, and her own fragrant warmth. She will place sweet grapes between her toes and, in her navel, a pale silver crescent pared from a white peach. Later, between her plump thighs he will discover a trove of glistening seeds from a ripe pomegranate. Laughing with delight, they will share these morsels, biting and sucking them one by one, savoring the juice as it glides, sweet and tart, from one mouth to another. What can there be of fearful doubt in such an hour? Yet Diane searches Henry's eyes searching her own; it is only in his eyes that she may study her true reflection— the tiny self that is dwarf to Diane, as Morgantina is dwarf to Catherine. The king's favorite cannot perceive what lurks behind the bright favorite in the king's eye; yet he need not perceive what may lurk behind the king in hers. In love's eye, the pupil is apt, though it learns scarcely more than can be spied in a looking-glass.

Henry's ardor is at its height; Diane knows only this— and allows it to persuade her that all may be well. Henry keeps his counsel this night; he blurts not a word of Cornelius, of the triumph he will soon taste, red and sweet as this lovers' juice, or even of the riches he will bring to Diane, to soothe her anxious heart. He has never before kept a secret in this bed of hers; this inflames him; his

134

passion feeds upon it; he is tireless; he will mount and mount again, riding her until, breathless and spent, she begs for surcease. What miracle is this? Freedom from Catherine; pregnant Catherine, she decides, and drifts into blissful sleep.

IN THE VERY HOUR OF DAWN, Cornelius, pacing in his rooms like a felon awaiting the hangman, is startled by a muffled knock at the door of his laboratory. It is the cloaked nobleman, he who came at the king's bidding for a treatment against night fears and failure of the virile member. The man's face is once more shadowed by his hooded robe, and he speaks in low, accented tones, as though to deceive himself—for surely he knows that Cornelius knows him. My powers are well restored, he says. Yet I suffer from a certain stiffness here, a pain there.

The head, the heart, murmurs Cornelius, lighting tapers, moving tapers, covering the narrow table, so that the king's face may lie in shadow.

The shoulder, the spine, says the king, climbing upon the table, closing his eyes.

The magician washes his hands with a fragrant tonic, and begins to prepare a new treatment. The king hears a rustling, a dry tearing of thin tissue. A sharp burning smell assaults his nostrils. In an instant, the magician has peeled shoes and stockings from the royal feet. It is a forbidden act to touch the king's naked person without permission. The king utters no sound.

Cornelius seizes the right foot and attacks the sole with both hands, as though he would throttle it like a snake.

135

A pinprick of hot pain pierces Henry's body, flashing upward like a streak of light; he is afire, yet he is not; it is only a pinpoint, not a flame; it does not spread; neither does it go out. And in the next instant, the pain subsides; it is transformed into a minuscule circle of sweetness, like the point at which pain becomes pleasure, such as women speak of when first impaled upon a lover.

Still the king lies silent. Now Cornelius grasps the left foot and attacks the bones that lie atop its arch. He seems to search for something—a hidden place, a soft and pliant valley of boneless flesh between this hard crest of bone and that. At last it is found; another pinprick of hot pain; it subsides at once, like the first. The king burns, yet he smolders not, nor is the sensation aught but strangely pleasant. The magician moves swiftly now, to the royal head, which he lifts, murmuring incantations, sounds without meaning. He rolls the head gently, like a ball upon a column. He holds it in one hand, and with the other reaches for the pelvic bone, the thigh, the knee, touching, pressing, lifting, like a sculptor molding his clay. At last he returns to the burning feet, and removes the source of fire.

Return when you wish, sire, he whispers, and vanishes. The king's eyes fly open; he remains still for a moment, gazing downward at his feet. They bear no marks. An image flickers before him, of a painting in his own chapel; the dead Christ wrapped in a shroud, blue-white, the color of chilled moonlight. The body lies stretched upon a narrow slab, poor ruined feet upturned, their soles facing outward, toward all who gaze upon him, while the head, obscure, recedes into distant shadow.

Henry shudders to dispel the image, wriggles his toes; the point of pain is muted like an echo. He swings both

136

legs to the floor and stands. The pain is there, receding still, or rather, he is aware of its presence but can no longer tell precisely where it is.

Cornelius has left him a phial of some amber liquid, and a poultice wrapped in a green fig and tied with a strip of blue silk. This object is to be hung by a leather thong about the neck, and worn while sleeping. It is the sort of thing the dwarf would prescribe for a woman's trouble. The king hesitates, grimacing. He will not be thought a fool, wearing a woman's charm, not even in sleep. He leaves the laboratory in haste, without taking these things.

DIANE CONTINUES TO VISIT the dwarf's quarters, at first in the hope of confirming her suspicion, that Morgantina is with child, while the queen is not. But the creature is both clever and wary, thanks to seven years of playing Catherine's game of who can tell. Since the magician's fateful visit, Morgantina must never again be taken by surprise. Now her ears are sharpened; they detect a footfall long before a visitor reaches the outer door to her secret stairway. She keeps her potions, her tinctures, in flasks marked *Ague* and *Plague*, so that none may guess their true content, or their purpose. Even her herb garden is transformed, lest a knowing visitor disturb the patch of inkberry, or the monkshood, or a certain bold coarse-leafed bush, entirely without beauty, its tiny purplish flowers crowded together in spikes, like the tails of frightened rats. Catmint now cowers in a corner, guarded by a troop of wild lupine, and the innocent sky-blue anchusa, from which the dwarf presses her magical wine, nestles now in discreet trails along the rock wall, shielded by great woolly stems of velvet dock. The secret powers of these plants may be known to Cornelius, but to no other here. Some are useful for a night's journey, such as Morgantina's mother used to take, with her laughing fair-haired friends, in the days before the wind turned, before the lighting of the fires. Morgantina's own time is coming, and Catherine grows restless with a fever of desire, a state of excitation and tremulous longing for she knows not what, though Morgantina knows.

THEY LIE TOGETHER in their accustomed way, head to toe, side by side yet far apart, upon Catherine's great bed, while Morgantina instructs the queen in the art of applying a certain salve. This one is not like the others, one must be generous with it, one's inward parts must glisten unseen. The hidden flower of a woman breathes and opens to the essence of other flowers, like unto like. They share all secrets, as the earth does, whispering what they know of seasons, of death and rebirth. Catherine takes the shining stuff upon her fingertips and touches her inward body, though it shrink from such trespass like the folding leaflets of the sensitive pea blossom.

Morgantina, swollen with her impossible secret burden, rolls to the farthest edge of the bed, and squeezes her eyes tight shut lest the queen's eyes find her watchful. In truth, she does not close them altogether; a dwarf has a way of seeing all, through very small openings.

The queen's fingers travel slowly over her own body,

making the motion of a circle. She feels a slight warmth, not unpleasant. It spreads over and within her, radiantly, like a true sun. In a moment it grows warmer still, nearly hot. She flings aside the coverlet; she tosses, writhes. She gleams with unnatural pearls of sweat, like a peasant woman. A soft moan escapes her—from one mouth or another. Who can tell, with a woman? The dwarf lies motionless, watching through the tiny openings of her tiny eyes; the queen is on a journey. Soon the dwarf will paint her thus, so that both may remember the way.

THE WAY TO SAINT PÉ is long and twisted, a distance of ten days' hard riding. From the rude village upward to the Source is a climb through nameless silent hills, their emerald flanks humped like the backs of laboring giants. A few poor houses cling to the hillsides at precarious angles, as though a careless hand had flung them there when the green stuff was soft, and they stuck fast as it hardened in the sun.

Seen from the village, the Source appeared to lie in the fold made by the meeting of two perfectly rounded hills, forming a triangle, like that formed by the thighs of an enormous sleeping woman. From the low-lying point of the triangle issued a pure stream like the waters of birth, flowing downward to the scattered farms and villages beneath.

If one paused at any place along the mountain road, and gazed straight upward, the thighs of the giantess appeared to move and shudder in the sun, while the flowing stream glinted in the blue-gold air like molten treasure.

The queen's carriage must pause often during the steep ascent, for a wheel splintered upon a sharp rock, for the stumbling of a fine sleek horse with shapely legs too slender for such rough terrain. The horses of Saint Pé are stunted and swaybacked, with short thick necks and great shaggy legs like unruly wild trees. None would dare mount such beasts; none would presume to own them. They seem prehistoric, horses not yet named nor tamed by men.

Catherine cranes her neck, turning to gape at every passing creature: great black-faced wild sheep glare back, balefully, and refuse to move from the royal path. The dwarf sits silent, unlacing her stays, breathing the air of the mountain as if it were freedom. In the long day's journeying from the village, they encounter no human soul. The flanks of their horses shine like wet black silk; the carriage lurches and careens dangerously toward the outward edge of the narrow path; if it should plummet, its precious cargo would vanish without trace on the treacherous silent hills, scarcely disturbing the peace of a thousand years.

Catherine is not at all weary, though she has not slept. She gazes wide-eyed upon the monstrous gnarled trees, the great rocks sharp as weapons, in her path, looming overhead; the carriage rises, almost vertical, horses straining, aiming higher and higher into the thin air. At last, the path ends altogether; an impenetrable wood confronts them. The horses stop, whinnying, pawing, alert. Catherine flings open the carriage door and alights. Under her cloak she wears rough breeches and doublet. Free of jewels and skirts and the hidden armor of noblewomen, she springs and leaps hurrying toward the patch of light that dances between the trees like a playful spirit. There is a clearing just beyond, she calls. The dwarf must clamber down and follow, first shedding her own heavy garments. Beneath them she too wears the garb of a peasant, soft yellow leather, artfully cut and sewn to display both her deforming burdens—the hump before and the one behind—as though she carried a pair of great golden balls, wondrous, much to be prized.

Catherine watches, amazed, as the creature lumbers toward her in a great rolling stride. The dwarf moves in her shadow, as always; they press forward, cautious now, bending and twisting low branches to make passage through the wood. Slowly the light expands before them, then around them, encompassing them, as though a trusted servant held a torch to guide their way.

At last they reach a clearing; in its center stands a great ring of boulders; another circle, larger boulders, caves yawning like mouths. It is as if they have come upon an immense choir of petrified minstrels, dumbstruck in the midst of song.

And indeed there is music, a great rhythmic hum drifting toward them from within the farthest caves. There are animals about; a flock of the black-faced sheep, a colony of the stunted wild horses, deer and ibex grazing near an immense shining lake, toads and salamanders, serpents, birds of every color.

We are here, says Catherine.

FROM THE MOUTH OF the farthest cave comes the loudest humming, a throbbing pattern of sound that resembles nothing so much as children's laughter set to music. As Catherine edges toward the source of it, a running man,

---

141

entirely naked, streaks across her path, nearly colliding with her. He bears a platter of raw meat upon his head. He does not pause, and seems not to see her. Indeed, he runs blindly, like one pursued. The thief, if thief he is, rushes toward one of the smaller caves and is swallowed up, with his platter of meat, into the darkness. At once the sound within that cave swells, until it is louder than the noise made by its neighbors. Morgantina smiles and nods at the queen, as though this is right and proper, as though she knows how it goes.

A butcher's boy? says Catherine. Late with provisions for some feast? But raw meat? Some debauchery?

A priestly healer, explains the dwarf. Someone is dying; the healer has gone to him. Naked, carrying the fresh flesh upon his crown. His own body radiates power to make the medicament work. A man's crown is the center of his power; surely *you* know that.

Stark madness, snaps the queen, entirely missing the dwarf's note of sarcasm.

Healing madness, amends the dwarf, with her air of authority.

The queen frowns, trying to decide which cave to enter. She does not say this aloud, yet Morgantina answers at once. That one, of course, she says, indicating the largest. Beyond it will be seen the fountain, and the crystal sphere—

Catherine sets off, obediently, without a slap, a pinch, or a cutting remark. Morgantina hides her merriment at this. And she notices that the queen is holding her talisman, the smooth stone, graven with ancient symbols, given her by the lady Diane. That won't help you here, she says.

The queen recovers herself and boxes the dwarf's ears. Still, she proceeds to the cave Morgantina has chosen.

Inside, all is dark, vast, shining. The place is empty,

yet the strange harmonious sound rises from the walls or hangs suspended in the space between them. Perhaps it is merely the echo of a sound that has died.

Queen and dwarf make their way through the great chamber, and descend as it slopes down, sharply, opening out to another large space, and another, vaster still. At last a gray light penetrates the darkness, and a fresh scent of moist morning air.

It is the fruitful moment, Morgantina whispers.

Blinking in the sudden light, Catherine shades her eyes with her hand. Before them, the ground rises, swells, erupts; a delicate fountain springs from it, tree-like, bearing luminous fruit as well as water raining gently from its branches. The air is tense, silent; over the fountain floats a crystalline sphere, shimmering in vaporous mist like a shy moon, a great transient bubble of sheer iridescent skin, untouchable, an emerging form, still liquid in some unseen mold.

The entire landscape is the color of water, that dry ghostly water which lifts from lakes in early morning, to curl about the hills in the shape of mist.

The queen ventures forward again, toward the fountain. As though at a signal, human figures, dozens, hundreds, rise from the pale earth. All are naked, glistening as though wet, moving slowly like dreamers waking. Their feet leave no marks upon the yielding clay, and they utter no sound. Yet they are purposeful; like dancers forming circles and squares, needing no leader to prompt their turnings, no music but the low humming sound that eddies about them. They drift toward the fountain like the mist itself drifting toward the distant hills, more and more of them, silent, rising up from the earth, pouring forth from the caves, from God knows where.

The fruitful moment, Morgantina says again. Look.

Wherever the waters of the fountain have touched the earth, trees and shrubs now sprout, bursting into leaf and flower; birds flit among the branches, singing. The moist clay beneath them is no longer gray but green, grassy, fragrant; the waters of the tree-fountain run silver, golden, like juice.

The ghostly figures kneel in silence and then rise, clasping hands, forming a great closed circle around a man and woman who stand at the base of the fountain, gazing upward at the fragile crystal globe. At the globe's center a dark spot appears, grows larger, yawns like a mouth; within it perches a feathered creature with unblinking yellow eyes.

The owl Sophia, says Morgantina. Keeper of mysteries.

Now the naked pair at the fountain sink to their knees in prayer or homage; their hands reach for each other, beseeching, caressing, touching every part, even their inward parts.

Catherine gasps. The two murmur low, inchoate sounds, humming, hymning.

Acclivitas, whispers Morgantina. The way to the heights.

The outward circle of naked figures now begins to move in unison with the couple; undulant hands, arms, mouths, members meet, join and part like the blind curving waves of an inland sea. Above them the fragile crystal globe trembles and appears to fill, then to seethe and foam, flash and sparkle—as though some sudden substance were forming, separating, transforming: an alchemy like the primal churning of the molten clay beneath.

Catherine's knees buckle; she would swoon, yet she cannot turn away from the spectacle. Captive silly women! she sputters, angrily, hoarsely. Fed by lust, making no difference between man and man. Letting each one to them, on the bare earth, in the sight of wild beasts.

God has given them members, replies the dwarf. But not a dwelling for shame.

At the sound of her voice, the figures in the circle pause in their dance, without alarm, like court attendants awaiting the queen's pleasure. Morgantina makes no motion; it is for the queen to step forward or back.

A long moment passes. Only the waters in the shimmering globe continue their mysterious churning, their phosphorescent foaming. Catherine gazes up into the dazzling light, then starts forward like one enchanted, into the circle of hands, limbs, mouths, members. In an instant she is everywhere, taking and taken, like a sacrament, illumined and transfigured; a holy figure, pale and roseate, her streaming hair glinting with motes of gold.

Morgantina stands apart, invisible, inviolable; in a moment she will draw forth her sable brushes, her umber paints, her bits of canvas, from the rough folds of her peasant's cloak. In a moment she will savor her accustomed dry taste of others' bitten fruits. But now, with a start, she sees the body of the queen soften and change its shape, blurring, slipping. With a start she feels a heat rising in her own blood, flowing upward like the enveloping mist, as though it too possessed some power to transform shadow into light. Such a heat, rising unbidden to the radiant globe above their heads, would shatter its skin like a soap bubble.

The dwarf has no name for this peculiar heat; in its movement it recalls the effect of that certain pungent wine she is accustomed to sip in her laboratory: the vivid sense of her stunted limbs elongating; the mysterious certainty of her body floating, free of its tormenting shape; the unfolding of her fierce secret beauty, visible, reflected in the shining arc behind her eyes. I, she whispers now, suddenly; the sound astonishes her; she has not meant to utter any sound. I. It is a prayer. Saying it, I, I, she stumbles forward, into the enclosing circle. At once the queen's hand is on her, and others, others. She flings out her own hands, knotted into fists, to ward them off, to force the burning heat of her limbs outward, through her fingertips. She is at once bodied, unbodied, touched, untouched. The queen's hand has a heat like her own. I, she cries, crushing the sound, bruising it against an unknown mouth. I; I.

THE KING HAS RISEN from Diane's bed, taking care not to wake her. This in itself is unusual; Diane rarely sleeps when the king is with her, but watches over him as a mother watches her firstborn child. This night has been different in many ways. For this night Henry has kept a silence full of secrets, and Diane, who tends his waking thoughts, who husbands them, forcing and pruning their growth into plots of every intricate design, has not discovered the sudden black flower growing wild between them in the dark. This night it is she who sleeps, and he who lies wakeful. In the bright morning Henry will have a powerful new magic at his command; Cornelius has promised it, without revealing its nature or its purpose. Magicians have designs of their own for the royal garden. Walled and protected by the king's fears, strange and wonderful plants grow and spread with amazing speed, flourishing in poor soil, in deep shade, in a climate of desperation.

146

So it is that Henry watches the reddening of this day in a fever of excitation and dread, while Cornelius, alone in his rooms, begins to sift a pile of smooth and jagged precious stones, to assemble his wands and sharpened sticks, to polish and cleanse his mirrors and balls of crystal. What the king requires is an infusion of courage, of conqueror's boldness, and more than these, of awe and trust for his new friend, advisor, healer, who will be, if all goes well, his chosen traveling companion for the historic leap into his own destiny.

CORNELIUS FROWNS IN CONCENTRATION; he must choose his mysteries well this day.

After an hour of deliberation, he is ready. One hundred gleaming stones lie before him upon the table: black and brown ones of powerful shape and size, of various depth and brilliance; others of indigo, vermilion, fire-orange, smoky and clear. He will create a magnificent mosaic to be laid upon the king's naked torso: clear, light pieces for the crown of his head; deeper shades over the heart and belly; powerful dark wands and arrowheads upon the sexual parts and downward to the royal loins. One golden, egg-shaped piece at the navel, a great dark one, like a birthmark, at the pubic bone, and sharp, tapered points, like swords, radiating downward, outward upon the thighs.

When the work is complete, the king will gaze into the magician's mirror, and behold the beauty and mystery of his image so adorned. Cornelius will say what he must, persuading the stones to release their ancient power to the king's mortal body. Together they will follow the pathway of magic as it flows from stone to flesh, cooling and warming, creating the great ruler who will evolve from Henry, eliciting the spirit of these very stones. Emperors, warriors, gods.

Cornelius places and replaces the stones, again, and yet again. Azurite here, the teacher crystals, Egyptian malachite marked with the rings of centuries; lapis for its royal blue, pulverized into an impalpable powder to paint the king's eyes, as the ancients did.

Henry arrives, wearing a furtive, agitated look. The magician says nothing, but places a shard of clear crystal in each of his hands, and leads him into the laboratory, which has been transformed into a cave of treasure. All about lie great fragments of jagged, glittering rock, purple, black, green; uncut gems, some large as boulders, sliced and hollowed to reveal their sparkling interior secrets. Candles flicker within the cavernous pieces, casting light and shadow in diverse colors; it is as if some angry god has hurled and smashed his wife's jewels in a fit of Olympian rage.

Henry's small, weak eyes grow round and large, glistening with astonishment. Whence comes such treasure?

From deep within the earth of your own land, buried there by ancient beings, wise men who knew the secret powers they held, and would keep such magic from evil hands.

Cornelius leads Henry to the center of the room; the table is gone, and in its place lie cushions covered in rich silks, heaped upon the floor, flanked by tall rocks whose rounded backs are gray and somber, like friar's hoods, and whose glittering faces, lit from within, are cut so that their colors seem to dance and reflect one another's beauty.

Henry is to remove all of his clothing, and to lie upon

148

the cushions. He hesitates; how shall the king lie naked and defenseless? Cornelius smiles and snuffs out the tapers within the stones at one end of the pallet. If the king's head lies there, in shadow, his face may be hidden from the magician's gaze. The tapers will be relit only at the end of their meeting, when the king is alone, so that he may gaze upon his reflection in the magician's mirror.

The king assents, closing his eyes. Cornelius places the precious stones with care, upon the body and head, upon the points of kingly power. Here the azurites, here the citrines, here the malachite and lapis, the dark smoked crystal, the clouded amethyst. As he places them, each by each, he tells the king its story. By the light of the invisible eye, he murmurs; by the fire of the heart's blood. The words mingle and blur in Henry's ears; the stones on his flesh grow warm, then cool. Cornelius' healing touch moves lightly over him, like his voice. Alexander, he intones. Caesar, Odysseus, Apollo. At last he places the final stone, a great flat ovoid of black obsidian, over the king's groin. Zeus, he whispers, bending close, closer still. Zeus. His warm breath touches the naked member of the king. It springs forth in answer, like the sword of a warrior. The magician appears to take no notice of this, but moves the stone to the base of the column, like an offering to a risen god. Henry, but for his member, lies perfectly still, though his breath quickens. Now he feels the voice of the magician in his ear, though he no longer hears his words. Time passes. Time passes.

I have removed the stones. Turn, sire, that we may heal the spine. The magician's hands are warm now, moist, fragrant. He administers a healing oil, which causes at once a burning and a chilling of the skin, as though it were inflamed from within while an icy hand followed the

149

fire with soothing caresses. Now the magician's fingers press lightly here, firmly there, tracing the column of Henry's spine, as a sculptor molds a clay torso upon its metal armature. At last he reaches the column's base, splays the fingers of one hand across the king's buttocks; the other hand strikes like a snake, then lies still. The king is invaded; something is planted within him, a seed or a stone, a string of seeds or stones. Warmth and drowsiness overtake him, a flood tide of dull pain or sharp pleasure.

Turn again, sire. Cornelius has removed the stones; he will arrange them a third time. Here, at the center of Henry's crown, here in the shape of a star upon his brow; encircling his eyes, at the base of his throat, in a diadem across his chest; then, in intricate formation, a line of march descending the torso to the groin, exploding outward like the rays of a dark, brilliant sun, fire-red, brown-gold, green-black. When he has completed the pattern, he places a pointed crystal in the king's right hand and the slender handle of a carved silver mirror in the left. At last, he relights the tapers at the king's head. Behold thy beauty, he murmurs. Affirm thy light.

Henry opens his eyes to the blazing pattern of light and color; he is transformed into a living mosaic, immortal, a god-hero of stone upon the wall of an ancient temple. The air of the chamber is pungent with burning—cedar, sage, incense. Their mingled perfumes drift about his nostrils; he inhales; at once he feels a tightening of unknown cords deep in his inward parts, as if they have taken hold of a treasure, as if they fear it will slip from his grasp.

150

DIANE WANDERS ALONE in her garden. Her thoughts are troubling. She bends to examine the new, exotic tulips, glorious ruffled creatures, pale and elegant as court ladies. Yesterday they stood erect and preening in their ruffs of pearly lace, arching their slender necks, stately on their fragile stalks. Now, after a night of wind and rain, they lie together in wild tangles, disheveled, lifeless as a heap of discarded mistresses in their sodden finery. Diane's sigh is rueful, pondering this image. She must have the bed cleared at once. Henry is always to be spared the sight, if not the cost, of her rare failures, her disappointments.

But how to fill the sudden vast space they will leave, like a gap in the smile of a beauty? She quickens her step, then stops abruptly, fingering the ring of keys at her waist, searching for the smallest one, lately acquired. It is the copy of another key, one she found in the dwarf's quarters, while Morgantina lay recovering from her mysterious malady. Unthinking, Diane borrowed the key and ordered its likeness forged; she knew at once the treasure it guarded. Behind the shrubbery that clung to the long stone wall circling the royal palace lay a little door; behind the door, the dwarf's wild garden, filled with unknown flowers and herbs, bushes, vines and trees. She hurries to the place, creeping behind the shrubs, searching with eyes and fingers; surely the little door will be hidden from casual view. It is a long wall, and the search is wearying. At last she finds what she seeks, almost invisible, behind a tangle of overgrown vines. The key fits, the door swings easily; she must kneel to enter. Then she rises, gazing in awe. Every medicinal and magical plant is here—even the ancient one that flowers in winter, secret ones that hide by day, those that withdraw at the step of a stranger, those that tremble if one draws near, yet lie still if they are watered with the blood of a woman's courses.

151

Diane's approach is stealthy, measured, yet all along her path tiny leaflets shudder and fold in upon themselves; they know the step of a trespasser. Now she pauses, gaping at a well-tended cluster of bold, coarse-leaved weeds, entirely without beauty; rattails, bearing insignificant dark flowers, rise in rude spikes from bushy stalks, demanding attention. Wonderful wild birds of every kind are here, feeding on their leaves.

In another spot are gathered dangerous greens, banes and cures, bellflowers and wild lupine for the queen's complexion, alyssum to soothe her rages, yellow poppy and iris for her troubled sleep, yarrow—for the king's thinning hair? For the weakness of his virile member? Diane smiles. Anchusa lies in red drifts about her feet; this she knows, from dregs in the dwarf's silver thimble, is for steeping in a certain wine, to color one's sleep with scarlet dreams.

Even the rock wall teems with secret lives; fragrant shooting stars, their petals pointing backward like the ears of frightened horses; fennel flowers, the cause, perhaps, of Catherine's remarkable sudden plumpness, masquerading as a belly filled with child.

But Diane cannot tarry longer, musing; she must summon the gardeners at once. By nightfall a field of these majestic blue spires must fill the bare spot in her own garden. Belle de Nuit for a border, and the dwarf delphiniums, tossing in the evening breeze like the sea creatures they were named for. Hurrying, she permits herself a grudging backward glance at a brilliant patch of sunlight in the shade, made by a great clump of soft bucket-of-gold and velvet dock, nestled in blankets of woolly leaf. Diane herself would never allow such intense golden hues in a garden. A vulgar brilliance; just the sort of thing Catherine would choose—as though a queen's garden must be filled with sun, even in rain.

Outside the wall, she opens her hand; she has absently plucked a sprig of some unknown blossom, shapely, white, and a few fragrant seeds. What mischief might one undertake with these? Was this a maddening herb? What was this delicate flower, the color of innocence? Dare she inhale its sweet fragrance? The scent alone might so intoxicate a woman that she would swoon into a lustful reverie—perhaps never to waken.

On an impulse, she runs to the riverbank, finds a sharp stone, crushes a single seed, and tosses the pulverized bits into the water, taking care to hold her hand in the stream until the traces are washed well away.

In a flashing instant a great silver fish leaps up from the water, then another follows, and another still—all leaping wildly as though in flight. She stares, amazed, as they thrash like a troupe of crazed acrobats, high in the air, then fall, crashing, bellies up, floating, still as corpses. She reaches out and seizes one in her bare hand. It is alive, yet it cannot move to save itself. A potent mischief, indeed.

She will need time to reflect upon what fate has meant by bringing such powers to her hand.

Meanwhile, there is more ordinary work to be done; the gardeners will need careful instruction. She must consider well which man to trust with the gathering of this harvest, which to warn of the hidden dangers. Roots entwined underground with those of tiny white lilies, whose own roots hold a deadly poison. Even the lupine poses a risk; some say their spires must never be disturbed, lest harm come to all.

But with care and good fortune, there will be a fine show this night in Diane's garden. A pageant of beautiful nocturnal moths will come to play for her guests—followed by a stately dance of night-flying butterflies and hummingbirds. Wild doves will gather to sip the secret nectar that pours from the slender petal goblets of the scarlet gilia—the flower that bloomed at the beginning of time. All the new plants will be arranged in a geometric pattern, in the form of the royal device: Henry in the arms of Diane and Catherine. Lit with fireworks and low torches, the night birds and butterflies will gather to feed, creating a living tapestry: Diane fastened to Henry, Catherine forward and reverse.

While the court gazes with wonder, Diane will return to the dwarf's garden. She is resolved now to find the magical root that must be there, the treasure always found in the secret gardens of the good women, the beautiful women. She knows now that it is there, hiding its lovely false face among innocent weeds. At night it will shine like a red star in the darkness; she must find and mark the glowing spot, so that it may be gathered the next day, root and all. She will consult the *Great Herball* in Henry's library, and learn the ancients' way of gathering this plant, whose magic is the most powerful of all. Beautiful little herb, soft mauve-white blossoms, golden apples . . . She remembers, in a flash, the stories of her childhood in which its magic wrought miracles, evil and good. A plant that grows only where the seed of a hanged man has spilled at the moment of his death, wetting the earth. Not that of an ordinary felon, either—but of an archthief, a pure youth who got his evil nature while still in his mother's womb. Diane must have the plant-root; she knows not why nor how it came to be here, for surely it is here, and no one has brought it. Perhaps it came through the building of her new bridge, in the turning of earth; spades delving into deep-buried soil, down and down to a place of ancient tortures and executions, a place of horror and pain, of violent death. But if this plant now springs to sudden life,

154

if fate has sent her to discover it, then, perhaps, when the root is in her grasp, will its purpose be made clear.

SHE NEEDS NO LIGHT, for the night is full of moon; the faint red glow is there, like a taper held in a ruby glass. She draws as close as she dares, then sinks to her knees, mindless of satins and gauze, of brambles and thorns. How to mark the spot? A trail, little stones, twigs, blossoms. In a fever she gathers what she can, breaking twigs, plucking berries. In her haste she pays no heed to what she plunders, innocent or dangerous, oozing juice that may enter a scratch, or the pricking point of a thorn. At last the job is done; in the daylight she may return to reap her reward.

As she hurries back along the riverbank, she feels light despite the weariness of her limbs. Though her feet retrace the same rough path of stones, she seems not to feel the cold, the hardness; seems not to touch the earth at all.

It is the wine I drank earlier, she thinks. It is the lateness of the hour, the fullness of the moon. But her hands are torn and bloodstained from her rough work, and she has touched she knows not what. No matter, she must steady her gaze; the way is here, or there. Soon, Henry will wonder at her absence. In the morning . . .

Presently she drifts into a darkness that glows red like a dangerous plant; she stumbles and falls, upward, or so it seems, and when at last she sinks into sleep, her gown crumpled like a shining black leaf upon the riverbank, her head garlanded with iris, she imagines that she is in her own silken bed, that Henry's head lies upon her breast, that he is reading aloud from the *Great Herball* by the winking light of a single candle flame, and that she, rising, begins to sway in a strange ritual dance around the shining root of a misshapen herb whose golden apples smell of death. Three circles she draws with a bright knife, deep in the earth around the magical plant. She turns her face away from the sun, cuts off the topmost part of the plant, then the center. But before she can free the root, she must dance slowly around it, reciting all she knows of the mysteries of love. She glances once at Henry, sprawled naked on her bed; his virile member is transformed into a corpse-colored flower—violet-veined, nested in a thatch of pale, hairy leaves. He gazes down upon himself and reads aloud from the book: All parts of the plant are dangerous and useful. Seed, root, flower, all contain what you fear, or what you require. He looks up, smiling. Circe, he says. All that you require if you would turn men into swine.

Diane in the dream laughs at this, a wild laughter that loosens her limbs and quickens her dance, a frenzied laughter that takes the shape of forbidden words, a cruel language of love without love, like the movements of her body, the violent mockery of love, the misshapen dance of the devil doll, the dance with which Morgantina the dwarf once shocked the court. In her dream, the lady Diane gives voice to it now: a foul stream of curses flows from her mouth; a lewd and perverse lyric, a vile ode to every part of her own body, the inward parts and the outward, the poisonous juices, the evil flowers, and the deadly fruit.

Demons take fright (Henry is reading now, from the text, without looking up) if one but behaves lewdly enough.

Diane's movements grow more frenzied still; her voice is shrill in her ears. Sweat pours from her body until she is slick, glistening like a newborn calf in the seafoam of its mother's womb.

———

Finally, a starving animal (Henry reads), a dog or a dwarf, may be tied to the root. A scrap of meat may be placed just out of its reach. When the creature strains toward the food, it must tear the dreadful root from its ancient grave. In an instant the hapless creature will die; bury it on the very spot from which the plant is ripped; the creature's life has been taken for yours. Bathe the root in wine, wrap it in silk, cover it with velvet, feed it good bread, and beware— (He falls silent.)

Diane pauses in her twisting and turning, to cast a startled glance at the king. He sleeps soundly; and where his manhood blooms, the peculiar flower has turned dark. It is a rusty purple now, bell-shaped, with a cluster of shining black berries. Henry's head drops, as if it is bowed by the sudden weight at his center. Bent in sleep or trance, his brow rests upon the page where he has stopped reading. Sleep transforms his face, or else it is the play of shadow cast by the dying candle, or by Diane herself. She draws closer; closer still. It is true: he bears a swinish face, this Henry, her Henry. A snout and tusks; coarse hair like wild grass, like the fell of some fierce animal. His sleeping breath makes a swinish sound, and has a swinish smell. The stub of melting candle spreads into a shape, fuming like the head of a demon on a torturer's spike. Henry's own head lolls. Diane leans over him and reads. *Furiale, mortiferum, hypnoticon, somniferum.* Murderer's berry, sorcerer's cherry.

She bends to gather the gleaming fruit that garlands the king's loins. Suddenly a hand seizes hers, reaching from behind her, wresting her fingers from the king's body. It is the magician's hand. He plucks a single berry from the cluster and crushes it against Diane's lips, releasing a thick juice of cloying sweetness, the color of ink or the dregs of wine. The sweetness assaults all of her senses; a scream escapes her throat; her throat is afire; her eyes stream with scalding tears that sear her face as they fall, leaving tracks like the quick trail of a wild fire, or of blood that leaps at the lash.

Henry! she screams. The sound is not a human cry. The beast in Henry's bed stirs, bares its pointed teeth, moans like one snared in a trapper's net. The hand of Cornelius holds him lightly. The corpse-flower springs from his center, bristling, filled with its sweet dark juice.

Henry— The wild dancer that is Diane that was Diane cries out again, but now makes no sound at all; her voice is burned away. She leaps a last great leap, she bounds like a creature raving, hurtling, fleeing fire, to the edge of a cliff, to fall into the chasm beneath, into darkness. In the moment of her fall she hears an unearthly sound, a cry of birth-pain or death. It is the scream of the magical plant yielding up its precious root, and the scream of the creature tied to it. Dog; bird; dwarf? She cannot tell. King and magician lie together, spattered with a dark, sweet substance.

THE SUN IS HIGH when Diane wakes, breathing the delicate scent of dying moonflowers. The Belle de Nuit will be invisible now, and the evening primroses—all closed, folded, satin petals shriveled like the skin of an old woman. She touches her face gingerly, as though for reassurance; the rustling movement of her sleeve startles her. How had she come here, beside the river, dressed in finery for a feast? No matter; she must attend to the dwarf's garden, find the markings of stones and twigs, the path to the magical plant, the buried treasure, dwaleberry, murderer's cherry, sinner's flower, torturer's root, herb of the good women, the beautiful women. She smiles at this, knowing well that the good woman is a sorceress, the beautiful woman a witch.

She catches up the hem of her skirt and begins to run along the riverbank, her hair streaming behind her in dark ribbons.

She reaches the dwarf's garden, still trembling, her head filled with vague troubling images, wisps of nightmares. Now the key in the lock, the tiny swinging door, the peaceful stillness within. But where is the path, the stones and twigs placed with such care to mark the treasure? Where are the circles she drew in the earth? And where the stump of the root itself? She searches closely, as closely as she dares; there is no sign. The place is swept clean of debris; her own men have done their work with care, carting off stray roots and boughs as she bade them, transporting stolen blossoms to their new beds in her own garden. Yet she warned them not to disturb the path, the markings; path, markings, all are gone. The magical root, the red star, the buried treasure—is it there still, or not there, or stolen by another thief, stealthier than the lady Diane? Who can tell? Dare she risk another night visit to find the red glow once more? Like some reckless night moth who thirsts for secret nectar in the long scarlet throat of a noxious weed? No. She will renounce this folly. She draws a breath, seizes her bright knife. Snip, snap; she fills her arms with pale yellow sunshine, a harvest of sweet alyssum to be brewed in a healing tea. She must restore her own unbalanced mind, and return to her proper labors. She locks the little door with care and hastens away, without looking back, as though the place itself now held

159

some sudden menace. Was it the will of fate, that vanished pathway? Had the plant itself destroyed her marking, to protect her? It is said that one who owns such a thing must lose all ease of mind, even as the holder of any dangerous power, even as a king. Is there not a constant sum of good fortune in this world—so that if Diane should wrongly acquire more than she has earned, some other must have less?

She quickens her step, shaking her head to clear it of such false piety. Yet the troubling thoughts follow each other, linked like a chain of dangers or the beads of a rosary. The owner of this magic root may not give it away; one may sell it only for less than one has paid. Owning it makes one invulnerable in battle, with a deadly aim in the use of all weapons, even the weapons of love. Likewise, all ills may be cured, even the ills of love, including those ills that devil the weak male member or the barren womb.

Yet danger lurks gleaming in the gold of any magical crown, if it be a stolen crown. And even if honestly got, the plant must be sold for less, and less again, until its price fall to the smallest coin of the realm. And at last, when no buyer can be bought, the thing must twine its limbs about its final master, and return with him into its earthen grave.

I am well rid of it, Diane says aloud. Rounding the wall of the palace, she surveys the two gardens, hers and Catherine's, side by side in the bright sun. The great wound lately left by her poor ruffled tulips is miraculously healed. And the queen has a new flounced border too, a delicate white drift of achillea, each flower showing a startling streak of scarlet at its center. One of Catherine's gardeners is there, shouldering a hoe. He sees the lady Diane; he doffs his hat, bows. What name has that fine yarrow? she calls. Cerise Queen, the man replies proudly. Its flower will outlast all others.

CORNELIUS HAS PREPARED a sheltered, sunny burial place, close to the river's edge, where the soil is sand, yet steeply banked, so that it drains well. In haste he begins to unwrap his prize, stripping off its velvet cloak, leaving only the thin silk gauze beneath. He holds it aloft, marveling at its ugliness. His heart strikes at his ribs like a captive bird. From his pocket he draws six seeds of the dragon's root that must be buried here in a single shallow grave, covered well by boughs of fragrant spruce. Then the root itself may be revealed, and its powers unleashed. He completes his task, and with trembling fingers unwinds the shining gauze, to gaze fully upon what God has given him. In truth it has the gnarled shape and unholy pallor of a cursed thing; its limbs are twisted and splayed like those of an ancient crone, a wanton; its face too is blurred and distorted, as if in lewd abandon. Devil doll. Holding it thus, Cornelius feels his hand grow moist, slippery; his palm is deviled by an itch. In fear he covers the thing again, with its thin protective veil. He must stop this unease, this quaking like a robber bridegroom. Invulnerable in battle, he cries aloud, to the blue air. Invulnerable to plague, to misfortune, to the poison charms of woman, to the false promises of kings. He pauses to draw breath. Cornelius! he shouts then, lustily, as though it were a battle cry. His name flies out upon the breeze that stirs the wild silver-green grasses at his feet. Master of all magic, he adds, lest there be doubt. The grasses bow before him, giving no argument.

HENRY HAS RECEIVED a polite message from the archbishop, who in turn has had a message from the Pope. Buried in the greetings, compliments, wishes for good health, lie a demand, a promise, and a threat. The Church is informed that pagan cults still practice heresies in the hillsides of the kingdom, openly, within the very precincts of the royal palace. These matters had been thought attended to. Indeed, had the king not given his word to the Holy Father, his wife's kinsman? Had the Holy Father misunderstood some detail? Was a bargain not sealed with jewels and gold, with promissory notes and expectations?

Idle time has passed, while deviltry spreads like plague in the countryside, under the crown's protection. Since Henry takes no action against his own enemies, the enemies of God and of Church law, the Church itself must interpose. Henry and Catherine are to be denounced on such a date, by such proclamation, from the pulpits of dutiful priests everywhere, from the papal throne itself. It is likely that Henry's creditors will seek to form holy alliances to assist the Church in discharging its rightful duties. Evil kingdoms are forfeit, as the property of witches and heretics is forfeit. The Pope, cousin to Henry's queen, and to his heirs (if any), regrets the need for extreme measures. But these are parlous times. The papal throne has its duties too, and its debts. God's will be done.

Henry sighs. As the magician has foretold, the time has come for a quick killing. But can he trust the bold whispers of a conjurer? Are the Brethren of the Free Spirit in truth a harmless band? Weak, unarmed, possessing vast hoards of treasure, ripe for plucking? Is this the propitious moment? Are the stars right?

He retires to his chapel to sort his thoughts and seek God's guidance. In prayer and fasting will the answers be revealed. A small troop of mercenaries, the Church to provide gold and blessings, a few days' hard riding . . . Henry hailed by the people; Henry, deliverer from evil. Witchcraft revealed, babies' graves desecrated, obscene rites, public burnings, decent Christians.

In an hour, Henry reaches the decision he must reach. His conscience is clear; his brow shines with holy purpose. God's will. Be done.

QUEEN AND DWARF ARE JOINED FAST in the fierce ecstatic dance, overtaken by the Free Spirit. The dwarf cries out; the queen's voice shrieks in chorus. Their bodies leap and curl, like consuming tongues of flame. The queen draws breath in a ragged rhythmic panting, like the startled gasp of a laboring woman. But it is the dwarf who labors, the dwarf whose unearthly piercing scream signals the tearing of flesh, the crushing of bone, the giving or taking of bloody life.

A new cry, sudden and sharp as a bright knife, rends the air between them, opening out like an echo in a cavern, spreading like the ring of wild dancers, ripples in water, moons. Such a shock of sound invades the body, setting invisible cords of flesh in motion, as if they were lute-strings plucked, thrummed, shuddering, broken.

163

Prince of air! a woman screams in sudden fear. King of wind and dreams! Whose voice is that? Queen, dwarf, mother, virgin, whore, witch. No matter; the birth is recorded. Court historians will be summoned; the horoscope cast; the poet will compose an ode, a sonnet, a cycle of madrigals, borrowing generously. Cornelius will pause in his labors upon the design for the king's new battle dress, to fix the propitious time for a round of feast days, so that the populace may rejoice, bringing suitable gifts of gold, silver, jewels.

SINCE THE BIRTH OF THE PRINCE, Morgantina the dwarf suffers a severe recurrence of her mysterious illness. Indeed, she hovers near death, and it is said that were it not for her joy in her new baby, the queen would be plunged in sorrow for the creature with whom she has shared such merry hours. Her Majesty, still recovering from the ordeal of a difficult birth, is herself in delicate health. Her physician, Cornelius, attends.

The king, much occupied with pressing matters of state, has received reports of continuing disturbances in the hills. Witch cults, banditry, desecration of graves. A state of siege is declared, the soldiery alerted, able-bodied men called to arms.

THE LADY DIANE VISITS the radiant young queen, her ill-gotten child, and the dwarf whose life hangs by the severed thread between them. The child is perfect, a great healthy red creature whose howls are so lusty that it is said they are heard by peasants toiling as far away as the royal vineyards, the dairy, the peach orchard. It is also said that the babe resembles neither king nor queen; all marvel at its wondrous thatch of hair, red-gold as new-minted coins, a color never seen on a royal babe in this kingdom, and surely never in the sunburnt native land of the dark little queen, his lady mother.

Diane's eyes are sharpened by these mysteries as the hawk's are sharpened by that brilliant fiery flower, the devil's paintbrush. Indeed, she is often spied with her eyes narrowed in thought (though never so narrow as to signify a care, or to carve a crease in that perfect brow). She spends the nights in study, learning the *Great Herball's* secret formulas, for healing, for harm.

Many in the court believe that the dwarf will soon die; Cornelius shakes his head gravely, despairing that any antidote can be found for the strange poison that devours her. He has ordered that her throat be tickled daily with a peacock's tail-feather, to force the noxious fluids out. She vomits a river of black bile, uttering no sound, and only the lady Diane suspects that this peacock feather is tipped with the poison; that Morgantina's real injury derives from another cause; that it is in fact a mortal inward wound caused by giving life to a child twice the size of the cradle that bore it.

The creature languishes, yet does not die; perhaps it has a tale to tell. And so the king's lady commences to tend the monster, while the queen's ladies tend the monster's child. Diane descends to the dwarf's quarters at dawn and at dusk, carrying secret draughts and tinctures, infusions brewed in the dwarf's own laboratory, herbs gathered from her own garden, powders to render harmless the powders fed to her by others. It is a small, secret war Diane wages, for a small, dangerous cause. If she is victorious, none will reward her. Surely not the queen, nor the magician, nor the king. Perhaps not even Morgantina herself.

THE HOUR OF HENRY'S own holy war draws closer; Cornelius has cast the horoscope and fixed the day. It will follow the round of joyful feasting, as bloodthirst follows potent wine. The king's armor is ready, and that of the troop of mercenaries. The soldiers will be garbed in gleaming black, the king in blazing silver, his shield and helmet richly carved with powerful symbols, surrounding the royal device, blazoned in gold. The crest of his visor bears a garland of strange spiky leaves, modeled upon a design of Cornelius' devising; the leaf is from no ordinary plant, but the magical secret root, the root of Cornelius' fortune. Diane finds the design ugly and crude, but the king trusts its power, and so the magician prevails. Diane feels a cold breeze, like the whisper of a blade, caressing the soft nape of her shapely neck. Time grows short, like the life of a dwarf.

THE ROYAL COUNCILLORS gather to consult with the king. Plans are devised for the feast day celebrating the birth of the prince: twice—no, thrice—the usual pageantry, masking, dances, jousting. His Majesty wishes to joust, in his splendid new armor. Banners, trumpets, a roll of drums. Henry is exultant.

But the king has not wielded a lance in tournament for many years. Has not ridden in bouts since his father lifted him astride his own black steed, in a child's suit of armor, sucking his finger and wailing like a girl, until the king his father leapt from the horse, applied his whip to the beast's flanks, and sent young Henry forth, into the thick. Thanks to his armor the child survived a lance wound in the leg; still, his father held his praise. Thereafter, Henry left off weeping, but rode still with his finger held fast in his mouth. And though Henry never again rode into battle, he grew exceedingly fond of ceremony, and of armor. The royal armorers fashioned his helmets with an elaborate device, to render one strip of metal movable; one aperture wider than the rest, in the forepart of the visor; one opening wide enough to accommodate the royal finger, curled like an unborn babe inside the royal mouth.

CORNELIUS, AT HENRY'S BIDDING, has asked the circle of bishops to request certain proofs of the Pope's blessing. In the matter of holy missions to restrain the practices of certain troublemakers, to bring malefactors to justice, to rid the land of pestilence, certain measures are to be taken, certain procedures followed, certain powers delegated, with the appropriate documents, implements, et cetera. The Pope's wishes in these matters have now been ascertained. Proofs of all misdeeds must be obtained and recorded, through the usual methods: accusation, interrogation, confession, punishment. The common people must be instructed to recognize their enemies, and to assist in all efforts to flush them out. A cleansing and instructive experience for all.

Convicted malefactors may be punished in public by the approved methods: burning, hanging, impaling upon a sharp-pointed instrument forced up into the anus, gouging of the eyes, disemboweling, breaking upon the wheel, removal of the tongue, beheading. The Church will furnish neither weapons nor gold for the king's soldiers, but certain instruments devised for the holy pursuit of God's truth may be fashioned by Henry's carpenters, ironmongers, smiths, in strict conformance with designs for these instruments approved by the Church for use in such endeavors. God's will be done.

Cornelius keeps the sheaf of drawings, engravings, and prints in his rooms; he studies them well, marveling at their beauty, their elegance. The restraining frame, the breast ripper, pincers carved and toothed like the head of a crocodile, the noisemaker's fife, the Judas cradle. Ah. He pauses with a wry smile, contemplating the heretic's fork. An iron collar with a simple rod, forked at both ends like the devil's own tongue. One pair of sharp prongs is speared into a heretic's throat, the other into his sternum. His head may then be drawn back or driven forward onto the spikes, until he may comfortably murmur: I recant.

Cornelius in his hot-blooded youth was once threatened with this device, for advancing an unwelcome theory as to the private life of the Virgin's mother. He recanted before the prongs of the fork were placed.

He sighs, turning the page. For preparing a witness prior to investigation, a special chair, studded with spikes upon all its inner surfaces, is recommended. Whosoever is seated may thus be pierced at once in every part of the body: arms, back, legs, buttocks. The question may then be put, with good hope of a quick and truthful reply.

Cornelius closes his eyes in thought, imagining a line of naked Brethren, held by restraining belts and punishment collars, awaiting instructions. He imagines a young woman stripped and tied, spread-limbed, to stakes upon an execution dock, while a powerfully built man lifts the great breaking-wheel; he raises it, straining, grunting, above his head, then lowers it with a righteous cry, crashing it down upon the delicate bones of the sinner at his feet. Each blow reduces a limb or joint to pulp, yet the mortal blow is withheld, so that she—so that Cornelius—may savor the destruction of her body as she has savored that of her soul.

The magician pauses in his reverie, conscious that his manhood has risen in holy wrath at this apparition; that his breath grows short, his body warm, his eyes glassy with righteous passion. Again the wheel of his mind rises and crashes down; what is left of the woman, of her mortal sins, of his own, twists and writhes before him like the limbs of a magical plant-root, a thing growing deep in the earth, shaped like a woman, in her infernal image.

God's will, he murmurs hoarsely, as if someone had demanded an explanation. He extinguishes the stub of candle beside him. In the dark, dogs come to devour the living mass that was the woman screaming. He can hear their tongues, their animal cries. Does this detail conform to the specifications of the code approved for investigations? The scholar does not need to look this up; he takes a righteous comfort in the certainty that he knows.

MORGANTINA'S EYES FLY OPEN, as though she starts from ordinary sleep. The lady Diane's cool fingers are touching her face, and the room is fragrant with sweet, heavy odors. The dwarf stirs, but her limbs do not move. There is no feeling anywhere in her lower body, not even pain. What have you done? she whispers fiercely to Diane.

I? says Diane. Only tended what others left to die.

The queen?

The queen is well, says Diane. The queen is with child. At last. Or, shall one say, again.

I have been on a journey, the dwarf murmurs, clearing wisps of memory from her mind.

On a most perilous, winding road, Diane replies, slyly. Especially in this weather. Drink this. She proffers a steaming draught in the dwarf's thimble.

Morgantina stares. But what has happened? Why am I thus?

Mortal wounds, poisons, enemies, friends. Diane smiles. Drink this.

The dwarf obeys, sipping cautiously. Then she reaches beneath the coverlet, gropes, explores, brings the hand forth, amazed. It is dyed red; her life ebbs through her fingers. She utters a low animal sound, a cry of fear. Diane presses a hand to the dwarf's mouth. You must not cry out, she says. Do not let your mistress find you much improved, lest I be accused of ministering black arts. Already the tongues of the court are in motion. Where does the lady Diane go in the afternoons?

Why should any think you come here? To me?

Diane does not reply to this. Instead she says: A dwarf is shaped like a question mark. She may die seeking the answer to her body. I too— She trails off, with a shrug.

But why save me? At such risk?

You may know a useful secret or two. Diane's tone is light: I have learned much that is already useful. From your garden. Your library. Your delirium.

Morgantina closes her eyes, sinks back upon her cushions. I know nothing, she protests. I have done nothing.

Diane leans over her. Did you not heed what I said? The queen is with child again. Is it another miracle? I would give much to know the truth of the first one.

Morgantina struggles to hold her tongue. Then she explodes in a rush: The child is born? Alive? Whole? Of . . . normal size?

Diane smiles. A great howling prince with red-gold locks, whose protests are heard all the night and day. His nurses despair of comforting him.

Nurses? Might I—?

Might you! laughs Diane.

Morgantina grows wary. O, she says, if the queen's dwarf could but play her merry pranks, they would soon bring a smile to a melancholy child. He is—you are certain he is whole? Perfect?

Diane nods, holds her arms wide, as though to cradle a babe of enormous size. Now rest, she says. Pray no one will come before supper. If Cornelius sends his poisoners, refuse the feather. Diane places a basin filled with clear fluid beside the bed. Show them this, in proof that the black bile is spent. And protect your inward parts with this ointment, lest the doctors bring a harmful salve. Heed me well, Morgantina; if they suffer you to live, your tongue endangers them all.

———————

And you as well, my lady? If you are seen to interfere? Diane, smiling, prepares to go. Who can tell? she says lightly. Is not the ending subject to change, as we are? She blows a kiss to the dwarf, bends and crouches until her head is low enough to clear the pointed arch of the secret doorway.

MORGANTINA ROLLS WITH DIFFICULTY to the edge of the bed, and lowers herself to the floor; she is too weak to stand without clinging to the bedpost. One foot ventures forth; she tries to trust it with her weight, closes her eyes, sways, fighting blackness. How to find strength to do what she must? Her painting awaits; her luminous chronicle of the queen's journey, the visit to the Brethren, the birth of the prince? How shall she persuade the queen and the magician to spare her life?

She sinks, swooning, back upon the bed—blood pooling within her, filling her, overflowing.

Presently the sound of sharp voices pierces the shadowy silence of her fitful dreaming. Cornelius, his henchmen, a new physician sent by Diane, with the king's permission. They poke and prod; hands hold her fast; the poison-tipped peacock quill brushes her lips. She turns her head. No; see there! Her voice is faint as the echo of a whisper. The fluid is clear, she gasps. I grow weak from this purging.

They examine the basin; they sniff; they argue. The new physician stays the hand that wields the feather. Cornelius relents; they leave her.

Quickly she anoints herself with Diane's salve. Then she gropes among the bedclothes. Within the hem of a

172

pillow slip, she has sewn her emergency vial of Seven Thieves' vinegar for the outward wounds. She rubs well. Here. And here. The inward parts require more drastic remedy. Even had she the strength for a night visit to her garden, Cornelius now posts a guard outside her door. No chance remains but to trust the lady Diane with certain errands. In restless sleep her thoughts conspire; her garden gleams and beckons. Young succory shoots forced in darkness, and the dwarf wild rose, its shining leaves so dark they seem not green at all but black. Seedlings of anchusa to treat the scarlet fancies, mingled with the dangerous juices of poppy and thornapple. She murmurs their names as though to summon them. The maddening herb—

Which one? whispers a voice in the darkness. The dwarf's eyes widen in fear, but it is only the lady Diane, who has heard her.

I know not, says Morgantina, crossly. I was dreaming.

Which maddening herb? Diane persists. The one whose juice the Maenads drank to set their eyes afire?

Fool's tales, sniffs the dwarf, in a contemptuous tone. A certain apple must be gathered, though. Bring me— she raises herself, pointing—paper for sketching, colors, soft brushes, inks.

Diane obeys in silence, like a serving maid, fetching all that the dwarf requires. Morgantina begins to paint her garden, each dark berry, each flower, seed, and root, portrayed in place, in the very spot where it will be found. These are not yet ripe, she says; they will be easy to gather. The spines of this are soft now; yet take care to avoid any that prick, any that resist the touch. Do not press a sweet or fragrant finger to the lips. Nor inhale deeply. A bee that feasts upon nectar from a single tube of this one gives a honey that kills in an instant.

Three fragrant apples from this, no bigger than walnuts, and a half inch of the root, no more. Fetch the smallest mortar from my laboratory—

Diane pales, horror-struck. You cannot mean to drink—

Morgantina laughs. I am very careful with potions. Three-twentieths of an ounce of this one makes the king a devil of a fellow. Twice that, and he has unseemly thoughts of the queen. Thrice as much would drive him permanently mad, and half an ounce will do for a murder. It is said the old king used it for spear poison, even in tournaments, when the wager was high enough.

But you? What will happen to you?

A dwarf may be driven perfectly mad for an hour on a scant thimbleful. Mad enough to persuade Cornelius that I know nothing of journeys, of Free Spirits or lewd delights. Mad enough to persuade Catherine that no monster's hand ever touched a queen, nor queen's lips kissed a monster.

Nothing of a child?

Nothing at all. All in fun, and no harm done.

Still Diane looks doubtful. The queen will not believe it. The magician will examine you in horrible ways. Tricksters know these tricks.

The dwarf hitches up her good shoulder, smiles, burrows deeper into her cushions, so that nothing of her is visible at all. If they know this one, she says, then I am done for. But I doubt that they do. This shrub grows only in the East; its powers are unknown here. Besides, there are a thousand pearls of great price hidden in the rooms of Cornelius. Some there are who would find that at least as amusing as the ravings of a dwarf.

Diane smiles. What a clever monster you are!

That makes at least two of us, replies Morgantina.

———

174

✳   ✳   ✳

IT IS GOSSIPED AMONG the serving women, the queen's ladies, that Catherine hates and fears the child. She will not suffer it to be held near her; indeed, she will not venture into the nursery unless the king is with her, and a circle of admiring strangers. The king, however, swelled with manly pride, visits often, bringing Cornelius or the lady Diane, though never both at once. The child's shock of flame-colored hair is no longer remarked on. Cornelius' own red-gold locks have turned a darker hue since the child's birth; this curiosity too goes unremarked. Even the lady Diane, who keeps such careful watch on the mysterious ways of her enemies, does not mention this to Henry. Cornelius' hair grows darker to suit his purposes, that is all.

URGENT LETTERS BETWEEN the king and the Church Fathers now flow steadily as the stream that links the royal palace to the distant city where the priestly powers are centered. All messages composed by Henry's councillors are subject to review and scrutiny by Cornelius, whose natural skills in plotting and scheming, whose learning in the pious arts of persuasion, continue to earn him the king's trust in these delicate matters. The court is advised that no secret deliberations in any sphere of activity may occur without the magician's participation. He is given new official titles: aide of the king's bedchamber; super-

175

visor of royal works; privy councillor; chamberlain; curator of the royal collections. It is said that he seeks knighthood in the highest military order; that Henry has promised it to him.

Still the lady Diane keeps her counsel, ministering to the king in the ways that are left to a woman when talk of warrior deeds fills the air around him. And in the darkening hours of the late afternoons, she ministers to the dwarf Morgantina. The creature shows little sign of recovery, but in truth her strength is much restored.

Each dawn she rises with the sun and resumes her secret labors, painting her chronicle of royal adventures upon strips of canvas to be sewn to the backs of magnificent tapestries, rolled and stored in hidden rooms filled with other treasures that are out of fashion, out of favor, out of the royal way. Here Morgantina's work will be safe; she may paint treason to her tiny heart's content, sparing no detail, no fantastic line or color.

She may portray the queen as Maenad, eyes afire, loosened hair streaming like dark water, naked limbs glistening in unearthly light. She may paint herself to the very life, her own monstrous shape swollen, contorted in impossible postures, knotted and joined with the queen's in livid tangles, like ancient statues of demon goddesses locked in mortal combat.

Heresies are here, gleaming like evil jewels. A single panel would suffice to send artist and subject alike to the stake, to the gallows; to be hanged by the feet, to be sawn in half by a toothsome blade.

As the sky reddens, Morgantina quits her scaffold, hides her work, and climbs exhausted upon her invalid's bed.

At noon the physicians come and go, shaking their

gray heads. Cornelius' visits are brief now; he has more pressing matters. And though the creature is slow to die, she seems no more to threaten him; he sees her smaller, weaker, fainter upon her pillows, a shadow of his vulnerable past.

The queen sends word that she will come this day, or surely the next. She does not come, however. Each day Diane reports that Catherine glows with new life; likewise, her red salon glows with brilliant talk and diverting games, cards and dice, masking, songs, visitors with astounding gossip. A new artist has come to finish the work in the salon—the Minerva portrait, a splendid group of statues, very chaste, the Virtues, for the rose garden. Feast days follow one upon another in a fevered round; there is scarcely a pause between celebrations for prayer, for contemplation, for the sewing of new gowns.

How does the child? asks Morgantina. Do they dote on it? Diane shrugs her shoulders. I fear it squalls overmuch. The queen looks forward to the new one; perhaps it will be sweeter-tempered. Perhaps it will bear a trace of the royal coloring. At these words, as though at a signal, the queen appears, crouching in the dwarf's doorway. How fares the creature? she demands, in a tone of ice. Diane would respond, but Morgantina, with a great effort, raises her monstrous head and wills her eyes to meet the piercing gaze of her mistress. What is that? she shrieks. Catherine flushes. Diane stammers, Why, why—but the queen signals with a warning finger and steps closer to the bed. How do you do? she says. I had quite forgot how ugly you are.

Caw, caw, the dwarf replies, politely.

Do you remember me? says Catherine, venturing a tiny vicious tweak of the creature's nose. The nose wrinkles in response, thoughtfully, as though it sniffs the air for a familiar scent.

What is that? the dwarf cries again. Hark, lady, did you not hear a rustle of feathers? It bit me! Here! Summon the guard; the parrots are uncaged!

Catherine is wearing a taffeta gown of green and gold; she is swollen to mountainous size. Indeed, the wits at court note well that in her first pregnancy (despite her artful pillowing) she grew no rounder than a slender girl after a modest feast, yet was delivered of a monstrous great babe. Now they wager, laughing merrily, on the measure of the giant that lurks within her this time.

Parrot! shrieks Morgantina. Bit me! She falls back in a deathly swoon, almost disappearing into her cushions.

Diane restrains her laughter, and whispers gravely to the queen of the dwarf's delirium, her loss of blood, her night terrors. Because of the damage to her inward parts—by the poisons, she adds, prudently—the creature can no longer fold her limbs into her famous sleeping posture. And thus she cannot rest.

What damage? snaps the queen.

The physicians say it is a common malady of the female organs. Common. A dwarf is subject—

Subject to the queen, snaps Catherine. This . . . delirium is most dangerous. I will have her cured of it at once.

Time for the maddening herb, whispers Morgantina, once the queen has safely squeezed her great green bulk through the tiny archway. It will take too long, says Diane. The dose must be adjusted accordingly. Morgantina proffers her thimble. Half a seed of the henbane. First set it alight. Bring me a pinch of the smoldering ash. Cover the thimble with a coin as you carry it, lest you breathe the fumes. Diane hastens to the garden, to the laboratory, and at last to the dwarf's bedside. Morgantina empties one thimble into another, stirs the contents with a hair of her own head, and drinks. Leave us now, she says, softly. Fear not.

DIANE MAKES HER WAY BACK, slowly, from the dwarf's quarters out into the sharp light of the courtyard. The two gardens, hers and Catherine's, glow like fire and moon, opposing, side by side. Beyond them lies the king's dark maze, dense, splendid, lightless. She is startled by a rush of tears upon her cheeks. Henry too must be fed a maddening potion: it is time. She turns her back upon the gardens and hurries to the king's chamber, sifting poisonous words in her mind, tasting them. The magician, the child, the flame-colored hair, the dwarf's illness, the stolen pearls, the queen's red rage.

Will he let her body comfort him in the old ways? In truth, Diane cannot answer this. Since his new trust in the magician holds him like a madness, her accustomed way to him is barred. On the nights he lies with her, something of him lies elsewhere. He visits Cornelius on the other nights, and in the days that follow he wears a face she does not know. Talk of devils and burnings fills his lips like the taste of potent wine, and his eyes shine with a lunatic light. His finger still flies to his mouth, to lie tightly curled within his cheek, else she would scarcely know it was Henry.

He smiles to see her; this much, at least, remains. He is wearing his new suit of armor. With a glittering clangor he turns to lunge at her shadow, a child's game. His laugh rings within his helmet, a harsh metal laugh.

O, but you are magnificent, says the lady Diane.

You really like it? Magnificent, really? The echo has a childish voice, wheedling. She knows this voice.

It makes you so . . . huge, she says. Terrifying.

You mean it? Terrifying? He lunges again, turns sharply to face his looking-glass, studies his pose. It *is* gorgeous. I'm going to joust in it, you know. Tomorrow.

You have decided, then.

Why not? He pushes the visor back and gazes at her, anger flickering. Don't you think I'll win?

She fixes her gaze upon him, meeting the challenge. If you must, then you will, as always. She smiles then, holding out both her hands. My dearest, bravest Henry.

I am a little nervous, he confides. But in this suit I move like lightning. Just look at the way these finger joints work; the man is a genius.

Truly. Diane stretches forth one admiring hand, touches the cuirass, strokes the breastplate. Mm. Who will be your challenger?

Cornelius. We've been practicing every day. For the expedition.

—Massacre of the Brethren? You're really going to do that? When?

He shrugs, uncomfortably. You heard, then. I thought I told you; it's all set for the Sabbath. While they are at their foul rituals. Hand me that other sword, will you? Watch this. He pivots, feints, dances backward. The suit moves upon him like shining water.

Diane shudders, though her smile is dazzling. O! She claps her hands like a thrilled child. O! She has come to speak of urgent matters, of lives and deaths. Yet she will hold her tongue. If the king will tilt lances with his magician, he must not know the truth of the contest until after he wins it.

SAFE IN HIS ROOMS, Cornelius has unwrapped his magical plant-root, bathed it in an excellent wine, fed it with hearty rough bread. Now he sits gazing at it, touching it with a lover's trembling fingertip. Invulnerable in battle, deadly aim in the use of weapons . . . yet the shape of it disturbs him still, arousing a feeling of dread, like a sickness. It is the way its limbs seem to twist, like the limbs of a woman, grotesque, writhing. In pain or ecstasy? Are they one and the same, in a woman? Is the peculiar yellow color of the thing more corpse-like now, by the light of his candle, than when he first unearthed it? Does it sweat, or do his own moist palms make it slip in his grasp? Quaking now, he wraps the hideous thing in its finery, his fingers fumbling with the strips of cloth, leaving it half exposed. He flings open his wardrobe, thrusts the root deep within it, gropes for a safer plaything to occupy his restless hand, and finds it. Hard, cool to the touch, polished: an iron pear. It is a torture instrument of remarkable beauty. He strokes its rounded flanks; a soothing moan escapes his throat, surprising him. He must rest from this agitation he suffers, yet his senses rise. The black pear gleams up at him, as though it would speak. He tests its stem, within which lies the concealed screw; he turns it; the fruit springs open at his command, its perfect crescents silent and powerful, capable of shattering a mouth, teeth, jaws; or the inmost parts of a man or woman. He

181

closes his eyes, listening to his breath. His body rises with it, but does not fall. Why not test the pear, now, upon his own body? The screw can be easily controlled, a gentle insertion of the pear, a sliding, a flowering within; no harm done. If all goes well he will share this fruit with the king. He prepares an unguent now, a salve. Yes. If all goes well, he will share this fruit with the king. Before the jousting. Brother to brother. Knight to sire. Flowering within.

T HE QUEEN'S PRECIOUS BEDSPREAD, strewn with pearls like the night sky, lies in a tattered heap upon the floor. Pearls roll and scatter in all directions, white eyes darting into dark corners, until the hushed chamber is a forest filled with frightened animals. False! All false! The queen's fabled rope, coiled upon its velvet cushion, sleeps within its golden casket, guarding its treachery like the serpent in Paradise. A worthless forgery. This day a trusted serving woman, inspired by the lady Diane, inquired, all innocent, when the queen had last examined her treasures; when summoned the catalogues, the records? At once the queen commanded a counting, a recounting, a weighing and a balancing of every relic, every jewel.

There is no doubt of the thievery. The serving woman has been interrogated; all the serving women. The treasurers themselves; a hundred guards and grooms. Catherine cannot dispel a certain image, the sound of a single pearl crashing, rolling upon a marble floor; Cornelius the necromancer hovers over the queen, his white hands poised, rigid, as though they held a priceless gift of magical air, of pure spirit over her entranced body. Pearl; how came it there, falling whence? Cornelius' startled look; Catherine's will to dispel the moment.

Now she reflects upon the siege of ironmongers, armorers; the magnificent new chargers in the royal stables. Cornelius and Henry, Henry and Cornelius. The child within her beats and pounds upon its prison bars, her yielding flesh. She touches the riotous spot with her hand until it grows still. She sighs and smiles. This child will rule; she will rule this child. This treasure at least is no forgery. This king is subject only to her.

Tomorrow there will be jousting. King and magician, masked in silver and black, exquisitely wrought, paid for with Catherine's purloined treasures. Magnificent horseflesh garbed in crimson velvet and threads of gold, woven with pledges on what remained in the queen's coffers. Why should this rankle so, suddenly? A queen's riches are to the king, as she is. The rest is ceremony. Yet she burns. And scattered gleaming pearls, a thousand thousand, stare up at her in the dark, bearing false witness to her rage.

Tomorrow there will be jousting.

MORGANTINA THE DWARF WAKES from a fortunate dream and summons her strength, as though she herself were summoned by the demon's call to harms. She must visit the magician, though not as she did once, long ago, when first she danced before him in the firelight and called forth his unholy desires. This night she must visit him unseen, to retrieve what he has stolen from her.

The *Great Herball* has told him nothing of how the

183

plant-root may be made to yield up its power. In vain, Cornelius has sought the secret in other obscure catalogues. His library is exhausted, and the king's, and the dwarf's, yet he is none the wiser. If Morgantina owns this knowledge, it lies buried deep, hidden in the words to a song her mother sang of her journeys, even of her last journey, until the flames danced her away.

In the hem of her pillow, beside the vial of Seven Thieves' vinegar, Morgantina keeps her mother's last gift, the ring of Gyges made of fixed mercury, set with a little stone found in a lapwing's nest. Morgantina has never worn it, though she well knows its purpose. Put it on the finger, gaze into a looking-glass; if you cannot see the ring, it is properly made. Turn the stone inward to grow invisible; turn it outward to resume a proper form.

Through her labyrinth of rat-holes and passageways, the dwarf makes her way to the magician. The ring of Gyges is on her finger, its stone turned inward, lest he wake to find her well enough to rummage among his evil treasures. After an hour of frantic searching, she finds what she seeks: the ghost-white plant-root, carelessly wrapped in its velvet winding sheet, glowing red in the dark of his wardrobe, its long twisted limbs splayed like those of a poor sinner stretched upon the rack.

Faint with her labors, her wounds, her desperate fears, she scuttles backward; she casts a fleeting glance upon the magician who lies unconscious upon his pallet, surrounded by metal tortures, maps, texts of war. The iron mouth-pear, its jaws open and glistening red, lies clutched in his own punishing hand, like the comforting teething rattle of a fretful child.

For love of a monster, she says, under her breath. But not the monster he fears.

———————

The sky has grown rose-colored before she is safely abed and rewarded with a dreamless sleep. The dollwort root lies with her, flesh to flesh, mute and twisted as a misbegotten babe. It is the dreadful human shape of the thing that sows fear among the common people, and even more among the great. Its mouth gapes, and its arm, elegantly curved in an orator's gesture, terminates in the hand of a beseeching child. The dwarf has left its swaddling clothes behind, in the magician's wardrobe, wrapped about another root of similar shape, but innocent of power.

The dragon doll has done its day's work this night, for the dwarf, invisible, singing softly in a tongue she does not know, has set its charm upon Cornelius' lance, upon the king's splendid helmet, upon the squalling flame-haired child in the royal nursery, and at the last, upon the festering inward wounds of Morgantina.

Her silver thimble, filled with the maddening potion, lies ready for the morning. She must hide the root, drink the foaming draught, await the physicians and this fateful day of royal games. For all their endings, she well knows, are subject to change.

THE DAY IS BRILLIANT, cloudless. Pennants fly like trails of bright smoke in the blue-gold air. Proud steeds, polished as the shields of their masters, lift their silver shoes like ladies dancing. In the new royal amphitheater, set like a jewel at a center point just beyond the two garden paths, the crowd flutters like a flock of splendid birds, white bosoms swelling over wisps of foaming lace, ruby crests and emerald throats lifted to the admiring light.

Below, in the lists, the clashing of new metal rings sharp as a discordant bellringers' chorus. Shouting squires jostle and sweat; plumed helmets rise and clatter into place; men vanish behind silver masks. Gods are here, for the hurling of thunderbolts.

Henry has risen to greet the crowd from the high center platform. He stands entwined by Catherine and the lady Diane, the royal device come to life. Catherine's eyes dart like sparrows, searching the field below for the magician's black mail, mounted upon a black prancing steed, black plumes puffed out like storm clouds. Scarcely an hour ago, Catherine paid a visit to the king's chapel, to consult his silver mirror, shaped like a goblet, ornamented with a devil's face. The mirror, Cornelius' gift to the king, must reveal both past and future. On this day Catherine lit a candle of human tallow, held the mirror above a basin of holy water, and awaited the message she sought upon the water's surface. By thy holiness, she whispered, by the virtue of my stainless name, show me who has stolen my treasure! Presently the water shimmered and whirled, giving a shrill whistling sound. The voice of Cornelius issued forth, in a watery cry, like that of a drowning man. It spoke in Latin: *Ecce enum veritatem*—Behold, then, the truth.

A wavering ghostly image then appeared: Cornelius himself, surrounded by black-robed priests, brandishing instruments of torture, wearing Henry's crown. In a red rage, Catherine hurled the cursed thing across the chapel, upsetting both the basin of holy water and the candle of human tallow. Velvet hangings on the altar leapt into flame, curled and blackened; then, as suddenly as it began, the fire hissed and died.

Catherine, trembling in anger and fear, hurried from

186

the chapel, leaving the shards of mirror glittering where they lay.

Now, still as stone but for her darting eyes, she searches the field before her; the colors blur; all sounds are one sound, a single roar like blood in a fevered brain. A knight falls; the roaring rises, echoes, swells, is transformed into a scream. The queen turns to meet the king's gaze; Henry is not beside her. Startled, she lifts her eyes, turns, gazes down again. The lady Diane, black clothes billowing about her like beating wings, is running or flying; her feet seem not to touch the stones or the earth.

The knight lying there on the ground, a shard of silver, draws the sun as to a mirror. His hand is curled tight against the visor of his helmet, as though to shield his naked face from a blow. Just above the hand rises a spear, ribboned in black, tall as three men. It fixes him to the ground like a stake driven through him, piercing the visor like a needle thrust through a skein of silk. Blood pools around the man's head, darkening the bright grass, and the silver mask that still hides him, as though it still protected him. The crowd is hushed but for the ragged circle of scurrying knights, squires, guardsmen upon the field, gathered about the body, leading the riderless horse. The lady Diane is among them; she hovers over the broken silver man; she is gently touching the hand that lies curled so tight against the visor; she is trying to dislodge it. A finger, wedged deep within his cheek, lies trapped by the point of the lance. Still the silver face hides the man and his wound. Men are pulling at the lance now; it is torn free. Blood and flesh rush from the hole; the visor is slashed away; the hole left by the lance is an eye, was an eye. The fallen knight is Henry. At last, Diane, kneeling upon the ground, in the lake of blood, her black

---

187

robes spread like a shroud, releases the finger from his mouth, closing the mailed fist over the blood-streaked hand.

Catherine sways, and is caught by strong arms; whispers of shock swirl around her like black plumes.

THE LADY DIANE DOES NOT WEEP, though her white hands, her black robes, glisten with the king's blood. At last she raises her head, stricken eyes searching the place where the queen had stood, watching; it is as well that Catherine is gone, ministers and ladies attending her. On the field the silver men disperse, issuing brusque commands. The sound of metal upon metal is muted now, as though all of it were coated with some thick, silencing substance. The sky has darkened. Men lean down to assist her; she will follow the king. The lance lies beside her; she gazes at its bloody point, flesh clinging to it, bits of hair and brain. She rises to her feet, refusing their proffered silver arms. She will walk alone, following after. Her robe is heavy, soaked, clinging to her as though she has been bathing in the river.

The crowd parts, allowing her to pass. Her mind is perfectly blank; faces, trees, spires of the palace appear etched against the blue morning, as though every line has been cut into it with acid. Her moon garden looms before her like a ghost; the word farewell comes to her lips unbidden. She is conscious of the ring of keys, heavy, depending from the encircling chain at her waist, a familiar burden soon to be lifted. She will walk with a lighter step, she thinks.

188

                    *   *   *

CORNELIUS HAS SHED HIS ARMOR for this audience
with Catherine. His painful duty, his account of the awful
events of this accursed day. He kneels before her, fearful
images racing through his mind. His own naked body,
upended, dangling, the ordeal of the saw, peasants pointing, laughing, goading the deadly carpenters; or impaled,
upon a long sharp point, the very point of his own lance,
the fateful weapon still adorned with his plumes, his spi-
raling black ribbons, still dripping red, forced now, upward, into his own body through its tenderest aperture.
Now again, a black hooded man wields his own precious
sword, its crystal pommel glittering like an evil eye, slic-
ing his belly, delving for his bowels. Horrified, delighted
eyes watch, greedily counting up the pieces of his body
that mount beside him into a shining pile, organs, genitals,
tongue, hands. At last the pile vanishes in a haze of blood,
as the sword point takes both his eyes.
    Majesty, he says, in a beggar's voice. How has it come
to pass that Catherine should loom over him now, this
puny girl whose body once lay trembling, trusting, beneath his magical hands? How has it come to be that
his body now cowers before her huge, distended bulk,
this grotesque female, swollen with the double power of
fecundity and a rightful crown? Suddenly the answer
swims before him like a dancing flame. The dwarf has
done this—all this. Yes; she, dying yet monstrously alive,
invulnerable, immune to the tearing of inward flesh, to
the birth of a child of impossible size, to death spells and
poison. She, grotesque, inhuman, the very shape of evil.

                    ———————

                        189

In the night she came to him, smeared her venom upon the point of his righteous lance, upon the king's impenetrable armor. . . . His voice rasps in his ear, rising shrill as a woman's; has he blurted all this, aloud?

The queen, expressionless, her face a mask, motions to her ministers. Cornelius is led away.

She withdraws to her private chapel, where the mysterious glowing triptych now stands as an altarpiece, drawing ruby and emerald light through stained-glass windows. She will pray for guidance. What must be done? Must she wage Henry's holy war against the Brethren; against all free spirits, against the secret truths of her own body? Henry's profitable, necessary war. The Pope has sent warning, threat, promise. The deaths of innocents are already paid for, with her own treasure. The king's ransom. Debts must be redeemed, gold is spent. Cornelius is a thief and a traitor. Cornelius planned all this, with unholy knowledge and simple ambition. What must she do with his dreadful gifts?

And what of the dwarf, rightful mother of that demon child in the royal nursery? What of the lady Diane; her house, her jewels, her cursed garden, all stolen from Catherine, all forfeit now; yet something stays her hand, she knows not why.

Her eyes are fixed upon the painted images she loves— the fountain of transparent flesh that bears a fruit in human shape, and from whose center springs pure water in crystal arcs, clearer than any she has ever tasted; the luminous naked figures that rise, flower-like, from the ground, and whose shining faces bear no hint of shame or guilt, but only startled innocence, like the faces of other creatures that fly and graze, fearless, around them. God gave them members, she says aloud, but not a dwelling for shame.

This painted place, these phantoms are real, alive, safe in the hills of this kingdom, as in the chamber of her heart, lest she betray them. Has she not seen them, danced among them, joined their fellowship for an hour, a night, a day? She knows not how to trust this truth of her body, lest it be a cheat of the devil. The Church would have them burn. Would have Cornelius light the pyre. Would have Henry steal their treasure. A profitable, necessary, simple little war; a thieving murder in any other name but God's.

The queen has her duty; the Pope has made it clear. She must first destroy that which binds her heart to these wretched creatures, cast out the weakness, the wickedness within her that finds them beautiful, that finds them kindred. Of course she must. Of course she will. Hunt down, destroy, lest they find her out, lest they denounce her, claiming her for their own. There—pointing, shouting—one of us! That one, she, danced with us, lay with us, sinned with us upon the bare green earth, damned her soul! She, with her monstrous creature, journeyed here, to the Source of all evil. Let her burn with us now.

With these wild thoughts, Catherine's dark face grows ghostly pale. She does not weep, but trembles, sinking to her knees like a penitent. Presently she is composed. Seizing a taper, she brings its flame tip close to the precious painting. Yet her hand hesitates; how destroy a masterwork that was, by God's grace, saved thrice from holy fire? Yet she must do it; it is a test; God wills it; Henry wills it; Henry is dead; the torch is passed; the child within her leaps and turns, like a mailed fist. At last she holds the flame tip steady, with both hands, there, against the right-hand corner of the first panel, the panel of creation. The dry wood ignites, cackling and hissing like voices. Flame tongues lick and curl, until the brilliant colors darken, until the figures leap and run as though in terror, as though in mortal pain, running together in the lewd, joyous pattern of their dance, their last, her last. A terrible sound of weeping strikes her ears in the empty chapel; her face is wet; the painting is destroyed.

Catherine will send the soldiers. She bows her head. One hand grips the penitent's rail before the altar. In the other hand she clutches a new magic talisman, which she carries now always about her. Contrived and fashioned by Cornelius, it is a compound of human blood, the blood of a he-goat, and precious metals fused together at a moment when all the stars and planets of her birth came together, signifying a second birth, a new beginning of her life.

The talisman has two faces, one showing the king of gods upon his throne, gazing into a magic mirror held by a demon. The other face shows Catherine herself as a naked Venus, surrounded by symbols of godly and demonic power.

Thy will be done, Catherine murmurs, piously kneeling, stroking her talisman. God or demon, whosoever hears a queen's prayers, hears her well.

She rises to go; her tears are dried, and all her questions answered.

BEHIND THE CERTAIN SMILE of the king's favorite lurks a certain doubt, a doubtful certainty. For it is always the eve of the morrow when her lover loves her not. The lady Diane has reigned twenty years in Henry's heart; her name is graven in marble, painted similes of her smile light the walls of the king's chapel, the banqueting hall, the blue salon, and every room of the royal palace, including the queen's bedchamber. Yet each day has she known what the next might bring. Therefore this day is like no other, is like all others. This day her place in history is subject to change. The queen must summon the royal ledger books, wherein every gift of Henry to Diane is scribed, and its value noted. Crown jewels, houses, works of art, keepsakes. Catherine will have need of these things; when a country is at war, a stranger's property is forfeit.

Unthinking, Diane turns her steps away from her own house, house not her own, and hastens instead to the secret passageway beneath the banqueting hall; in all this day she has not once thought of Morgantina. Now she is seized with fear for the dwarf's life. Cornelius and the physicians paid their visit before the tournament, to find the creature in her maddened state.

Mad she was, and gave them a terrific fright. Seeing Cornelius, she shrieked and clawed at her bedcovers. Who is that cunning man, that one there, who turns his naked back and bids me ride him?

The men avoided one another's eyes. With a brisk motion, Cornelius stripped away the dwarf's covers, her bandages. No stains of blood were there; how could that be? How could her inward parts have healed in the night? Cornelius grew pale and laid his hand upon her. The creature twisted and moaned beneath his touch. Spitting, hissing, a stream of fierce words issuing from her mouth, in unknown tongues, in voices not hers, voices of men, of aged crones, of animals.

Could it be, the learned men wondered, that the poison had left the body only to invade the brain? Cornelius bade two of his colleagues hold her clawing hands above her head; at his command, the others poked and prodded, pinched and delved and pummeled.

Do you dare insult the queen? she shrieked. Where is my gold-crowned prince?

How long had she been thus? But yesterday she was aright. Guards were summoned and questioned closely; none had come in the night; the creature had eaten nothing, drunk nothing, nor moved from the bed. Yet she had been thus since dawn, moaning, shrieking, rending her night clothes and bandages, biting at her own flesh.

That one, there! she screamed, whenever Cornelius drew near. And sent a stream of toads and lizards from her mouth, splattering the young doctor who stood closest to her. Danced with me, he did, naked, at the mouth of the cave, at the Source, enticing my inward parts! Bestarbarto! Where is my gold-crowned prince? The devil has the fruits!

She must be restrained, said Cornelius, recovering his composure. The young doctor who was splattered brushed at his clothes, as though they were cursed.

Unbalanced mind, nodded another. I have had marvelous luck with a tincture.

Enula campana—two or three drachms should do it, ventured a third.

Cornelius shook his head. This is plague, he whispered. The others edged cautiously away from their splattered colleague. Such a fever is borne in the very air, Cornelius went on. Burn the linens, and all loose objects near the bed. Anything the creature may have touched in the night.

That one—there! raged Morgantina, commencing her thrashing and twisting.

Cornelius sent for the restraining frame, and the iron gag for her mouth. A small hole in the metal box would allow for the passage of air, but no disturbing sounds. As for the frame, it was to be fitted to her ankles, neck, and wrists; her hands joined palm to palm as though in restful prayer; her knees drawn up and locked in place.

Diane finds her thus, her body neatly folded upon itself, still as a marble death-figure upon the tomb of an obedient child. With a gasp of fury, Diane flies at the padlocks, wrenching and twisting at the ingenious shafts. Morgantina utters a soft moan, gesturing with her eyes. Key? Knife? What magic tool may spring open such a cage? What power? What curses? The room is bare as a monkish cell, swept clean of vials, caskets, anything a witch might use to free herself.

In their shackles, the creature's tiny praying hands lie still, palm to palm. Yet the fingers move; the smallest one bears a tiny ring of a dark, insignificant metal, set with a dull stone. As the finger flutters against its neighbor, rubbing and tapping like the fingers of a pipe strumming a silent flute, the ring commences to turn. Diane's stricken eyes follow the movement of the fingers, though she sees no ring, sees no turning of a stone. At last the fingers cease their fluttering; the stone is turned inward. Diane stares, the fingers are gone, and the praying hands, and the creature itself. The locked metal frame lies empty upon the bed, and the cruel iron gag, in place, suspended.

With a joyous cry, Diane reaches forth a hand; the dwarf is there, warm to her touch, yet vanished. Quickly she gathers up the cage, folds it in her cloak; in truth the creature weighs little more than the cage itself. Diane makes her way back the way she came, up the secret stair, through the narrow passage, along the great corridor to her house. There, with pick and silver needles, tools from her garden, pins from her hair, she pries open the locks. In an instant Morgantina stands before her, perfectly sane, whole, full-fleshed. I cannot stay, she says. The king—

195

The king is dead, says Diane softly. An accident; the joust; the magician's lance. It was— She breaks off, words catching her throat. Then she says simply: The queen has urgent need of my sudden absence from court.

Morgantina is strangely silent at this flood of news. Perhaps she is stunned.

After a moment, Diane continues: The queen will let me keep one house, I think. One house sufficiently far. In exchange for my quick removal. And my silence. And the jewels. She does not know quite all that I possess. I have already ordered the gold melted into bricks; she shall have a chest of bullion. As for the words of love they bore, the mottoes graven, those do I have, and shall I keep forever. Diane holds her hand to her heart, falls silent.

Morgantina reaches up and clasps that hand, saying nothing.

If you can do your vanishing act one more time, says Diane, I can give you safe escort out of here.

The dwarf shakes her head. Thanks, but I cannot go. She has not expected to say this. My life is here, if the queen will spare it. The child, my paintings—

Diane's eyes widen with amazement. You would stay? While Cornelius lives?

I suspect Cornelius has lost . . . credibility. The dwarf's good shoulder hitches up, her old playful gesture. She smiles. But who can tell?

CATHERINE VISITS CORNELIUS in the new dungeon beneath her red salon, where he dangles by his heels, listening to the music and laughter of her favored guests.

Every sound echoes through the cold stones of his cell walls.

Thief, traitor, she greets him, pleasantly. Sorcerer, heretic. The people cry for the sight of you in the hanging cage. What instructive pleasure for the young. To see those bloody instruments of yours put to perfect use. You yourself could demonstrate each in turn. Children, sucking sweetmeats, held high upon their fathers' shoulders, straining to watch the turn of the screw, the piercing of the spikes, the locking of branks upon your head. I like the devil's mask, especially.

Majesty. With a great effort, Cornelius speaks, fastening his inverted gaze upon her feet, the hem of her splendid new black robe. I have never betrayed your trust, he says. Nor the king's. I swear it. Others, out of envy or greed, sought to plant the seed of doubt within your gracious heart. An evil magic caused the king to fall. It was I who warned of the fault in his helmet's design. The armorer himself will bear me out.

Enough, cries Catherine. No witnesses need be called to prove your treachery. She bends down to the level of his eyes, holds out her hand, palm upturned. A single lustrous pearl rests there, its creamy skin iridescent in the stony gloom.

Then why am I still alive? cries Cornelius.

The queen does not reply directly to this, but rises, seeming to muse aloud to herself. Most useful, she says, the chastened servant who sleeps with a blade stroking his throat.

Then she summons the guard to cut the magician down. He will lead the charge against the crown's enemies. His honors and titles will be restored to him. He will pursue all designated demons, gather treasure, supervise torture and burnings, all in the name of Catherine, regent, guardian of the crown prince; and the Church; and the people.

And to all your unholy fevers, she adds, pausing at the bars of his cell door, you will add the cold fever of dread. You serve no devil now but Catherine.

IN THE DWARF'S QUARTERS, Morgantina completes a remarkable series of works, to present to the queen in commemoration of the new prince's birth. None can guess how she got the gold to glitter in her shining tree of Paradise, for she works now in the dark, cloistered in her quarters, using the oil of a votary lamp to mix her colors, and only the image of herself, in a looking-glass, for her models. The queen appears as Salome, as Esther, as Judith; haloed, winged, draped with transparent veil. The lady Diane appears armed with bow and arrow, shod in winged sandals, crowned with leaves. The dwarf herself can be seen in many forms—human, animal, bird, spirit. Everywhere her face is enigmatic, gazing out, gazing inward, reflecting upon her own reflection in magnifying glasses, in bubbles, jewels, coins, vessels, in the shining scales of leaping fish.

At last the queen descends the secret stair to examine the works. She has not seen the creature herself since the day of her reported madness, and the king's death.

You are well, then? Catherine says. I was told you were still raving, and near death.

The dwarf smiles, curtsies. I am both, Majesty. Else how would I serve my queen in her time of grief and glory?

The queen is not amused. It is said you have a new

198

friend at court, one who is no friend of mine. She cuffs the creature's ear, for old times' sake.

Oh, her, says Morgantina, lightly. What's become of her?

Catherine gestures vaguely. Even here, in the dwarf's quarters, the floor is incised with the royal device. Catherine's slender foot is planted on it now: Diane embracing Henry, while Catherine holds him fast. She's around, says the queen. I have not come to talk about her. I have come to see some murals.

In silence the dwarf rummages about in the storeroom, rolls rugs and tapestries into the bedchamber, assembles the strips of canvas. A splendid panorama unfolds. The queen stares, amazed. Where did you learn to do this? How?

Wherever, says the dwarf, with a modest shrug. However.

Well, says the queen. Fancy.

Yes, says the dwarf.

This one, of course, doesn't look a bit like me. The queen, on her knees, squints up her eyes like a critic. The vermilion in that dress, there, makes my skin look green. And you need to fix those pearls—there. Is that supposed to be you? Where's your hump?

I wasn't wearing it that night. Don't you remember?

Catherine tosses her a curious look, sidelong. Followed by a resounding thump upon the hump in question. Reassured, she resumes her fascinated study of the paintings.

What are these funny little birds?

Saint Pé chickens, the dwarf replies, carefully. They are very small and ugly, but useful. Much prized. Especially for the hatching of eggs of other, more splendid, chickens.

***

Why are they lying about everywhere, like dark splotches upon the landscape?

That is what they do, Majesty. Flatten themselves and spread out, covering more eggs at once than any hen of normal size. When they spread out, their heads disappear into their bodies. And they are fierce; none dares approach to harm the eggs they guard.

Hmm, says the queen; nothing more. But the message is not lost on her. She changes the subject. What is this little tree you have planted in every scene? Even here, outside the palace windows. We have no such tree.

Morgantina smiles. Artistic license. That is the dwarf pomegranate. Its fruit is smooth and silken, like any of normal size. But the dwarf blooms apart; its fruit is not eaten.

I see, says Catherine. Yes. Well, these are quite . . . interesting. I'll have them moved upstairs, to hang in the red salon. Strozzi will write an ode. You'll be as immortal as a dwarf can get.

Morgantina drops a curtsy and murmurs, very softly, Who can tell?

IN THE DAYS TO COME, scholars and historians who visit Catherine's red salon make much of the paintings, marveling at the brilliant colors; the bold, sure strokes of the brush; the freak of nature that created Morgantina, yet gave her the power to create beauty greater than nature's own.

In time, of course, the signatures are removed, and the work credited to Cornelius Agrippa, legendary artist and military adventurer who served as astrologer, poet, architect, and knight-errant at Henry's court, and who died in battle, of a poisoned spear wound, after a waxen image of the queen was found in his rooms.

The famous panel upon which Catherine appeared as a Maenad, dancing with a dwarf, is missing at the time the works are sold to a wealthy private collector, in exchange for a magnificent rope of pearls.

Gossips who feed on the scraps of truth about life at court say that the lady Diane left the palace on a moonless night, taking with her only those gifts of the king for which there was no record in the royal ledgers. Catherine gave her the deed to a castle in the south, perched high upon a stony cliff, with a view of the sea. The barren sand there had never nourished tree or flower, yet within a week of Diane's arrival, a garden was seen to bloom, more beautiful than any the lady had ever made, including her moon garden at the king's palace. Some there were who called it a witch's garden, filled with night-blooming poison plants that kept her young and beautiful though she was said to be ninety-two years old.

As for the dwarf, there are differing accounts. Some say the queen traded her for six others of her kind, three male and three female, who could be bred for profit. A kitchen-maid swore the creature had been packed inside a scooped-out wheel of cheese, and delivered to the house of a gentleman, in exchange for a barrel of monkeys, which the queen thought would be more fun.

But the most persistent rumor, one which serious historians now credit, is that Morgantina, using her magical plant-root, her ring of invisibility, and a certain handful of seeds from the garden, made off with the scandalous portrait of queen and dwarf, and sold it to a dealer of antiquities for an untidy profit, enough to live out her days in a charming thatched cottage near the sloping hillsides of Saint Pé.

It is said that the house still stands, half hidden behind a grove of dwarf pomegranate trees. If you find it, remember that the fruit, red and silken-smooth, is not to be eaten. Remember, too, that the ending is subject to change.

————